DEREK HEATH

DAY OF THE MUMMY

POPE LICK PRESS
2024

Prelude

The boy watched his father leave for work, listening to the dull crunch of rubber on gravel as he stared blankly through the greasy panes of his bedroom window. Pale morning sunlight peeled across the street below and he let out his breath, fogging up the glass.

The Mercedes cruised gently down the street and disappeared beyond the terraces, and the boy turned back to his bedroom. His eyes fell almost immediately on the desk, an old second-hand writing table from some school hall in the village.

In a small cage on the desk, a tiny white mouse lay dead, moveless.

Downstairs the boy could hear his mother on the telephone, already talking to clients. His sister, somewhere in the house, would be brushing her hair and getting dressed.

Slowly the boy moved to the desk and raised a trembling hand.

The mouse stared up at him with blank, dull eyes,

appearing to watch as the child moved his wrist in a slow circle, clutching and relaxing his fingers.

After a minute, the boy lowered his hand and sighed. Nothing had happened.

Nothing ever did.

Chapter 1

It took twelve of the men from the warehouse to winch the crate down from the back of the PortEx lorry and onto the cool tarmac of the museum courtyard. Yellow beams of mid-spring sunlight pealed over the roof of the warehouse and gleamed off the iron rivulets across the lid of the enormous, wooden container. It was only a little over eight feet high and about twice the width of a man, but the contents were exceptionally heavy.

Dr Andrea Cain watched anxiously from the warehouse door as the men, dressed in jeans and EHM hi-viz vests, carefully eased the crate onto a low-loader and began to guide it in her direction. The foreman, a burly dark-skinned figure with close-cropped hair and a sweaty grey t-shirt under his vest, pulled the trolley; the others huddled around the crate and steadied it with their hands and elbows as it passed into the dim grey shadow of the museum building. Stencilled on the side in faded red were the words *This Way Up* and, beneath them, *England*. It had been sent from Los Mochis in

Mexico, stopping only at the Charlottetown Airport on Prince Edward Island before coming directly to Gatwick. Andrea had been tracking it with a growing, niggling sense of unease for the last few days, certain that something would go wrong – that the cargo plane would be hijacked at Charlottetown while it refuelled, or that the freight lorry would tip over between the airport and the English Historical Museum – but now it was here, right in front of her. And though she was still confident that it could all go wrong (what if the low-loader somehow buckled suddenly and it crashed open right before her eyes?) she was excited at the prospect of finally getting her hands on what was inside.

Figuratively speaking, at least.

'Where d'you want it, boss?' the man pulling the low-loader called. He'd been foreman for a good dozen years, knew the layout of the warehouse inch by inch and had probably designated a four-by-four spot for the crate as soon as he'd laid eyes on it; still, he asked, and she thought that was nice.

'Wherever you like,' she called back. A soft breeze ruffled the black mess of her fringe and she reached up to swipe it from her face. Her fingers were arthritic and bent painfully into hooks; it was particularly bad today. 'You know me, I'm not fussy.'

'This one's going straight upstairs, is it?' he said, gently easing the low-loader over a tiny ridge in the concrete threshold of the warehouse. Andrea noticed one of the other men tensing, splaying his hand absolutely flat across the panels of the crate to keep it steady, and her heart jumped briefly into her mouth, but it was soon righted. Just feet from her now. She could smell horsehair and cedar wood. How long had she been waiting for this now? Weeks? Months? When had she first received Phillips' e-mail? First seen the photographs? God, it felt like an age had passed.

'Not upstairs yet, Karl, no,' she shook her head, 'I'd like to take a look at it first. Is there any chance it could stay down here for a week or so before it goes on display?'

The foreman shrugged. 'Fine by me, boss. I'll get it checked in and run it over to Storage Three, if that's all right. You give me half an hour, and it's all yours.'

The PortEx lorry swayed gently on its axels as more men and women in fluorescent vests unpacked and unloaded the rest of its contents. Andrea's eyes flickered from the crate to the truck: up in the cab, the driver flicked lazily through a newspaper while he ate a foil-wrapped baguette. Figures in orange and blue flowed into and out of the lorry, up and down a long steel ramp that extended from within down onto the tarmac, carrying smaller crates and cardboard boxes into the main warehouse.

Shadows swelled and waned inside the lorry, pooling over the angular frames of more boxes and oozing down the walls. Andrea shivered as the low-loader came past her, the wheels trundling loudly over concrete as hay rustled inside. When it had passed, and the lorry was in view again, she saw a young woman in a hi-viz and black combat trousers step out of the truck with a long, bubble-wrapped bundle in her arms. It looked like a long wooden pole had been swaddled in cellophane and a flamboyant excess of parcel-tape wound around it at either end; through a sliver of translucent wrapping, right at the top of the staff, she caught a glimpse of something shining and emerald-green, like the muffled glow of a jewel in the sunlight.

'Sounds good,' Andrea said absent-mindedly. Quickly, she poked her fingers into the waistband of her skirt and made sure her blouse was tucked in before reaching up to gingerly touch the pendant around her neck. Something inexplicable was making her antsy; the usually-comforting presence of the necklace did little to calm her. 'Thank you.'

As the crate was wheeled deeper into the warehouse, she stepped out onto the courtyard and headed for the lorry, raising a hand to catch the young, Black woman's attention. The woman stepped carefully off the ramp and glanced up in Andrea's direction. 'Morning, Ms Cain. *Dr* Cain, sorry. What can I do for you?'

Andrea smiled. 'Rachel, isn't it? I thought you were working with Dr Phillips on the new Boudica exhibition?'

Rachel stood the long, bubble-wrapped parcel gently on its end beside her, propping it up with her left hand as she extended her right for Andrea to shake. 'Good to see you again,' she said, her eyes flashing bright blue in the sun. 'You know what Pete's like. I'm less an extra pair of hands up there, and more a… well, an annoyance. Thought I'd come down here and unpack some of his old Roman exhibits for a bit, let him figure things out without me upstairs.'

'He yelled at you, didn't he?'

'He did,' Rachel nodded, tucking a loose wave of brown hair behind her ear and picking up the staff again. 'Oh, big time.'

'Don't let it get to you,' Andrea smiled. 'Whatever plans he's got for Boudica, he's not really the type to let anybody else in on them. *Especially* if they're trying to help.'

'I got that impression. Still, there's plenty of things for him down here, so at least I'm doing some good.'

'I should think so.' Andrea's smile turned to a frown as she nodded at the bundle in Rachel's arms. 'That's not one of Boudica's, though, is it?'

'Nope, think this belongs to you,' the younger woman said, looking down at a printed note taped to the package. She nodded. 'Yeah, looks like another one for *Mysteries of the Ancient World*. Love that. What is it, then?'

'Exactly what I'm looking for. D'you mind?'

'Not at all.'

Andrea took the staff awkwardly, wincing at the unexpected weight of the thing. Holding it upright, she glanced up toward its top; there was that flash of green, just a tiny spark of colour beneath layers of plastic protection. 'Perfect,' she said. 'Is this ready for me to take it up to the office?'

'It is now, professor,' Rachel said, gently ripping off the delivery note. 'I'll hand this to the guys and they can get it booked in. All yours.'

'Thanks. Tell you what, I'll have a word with Phillips when I get back upstairs. See if I can get him to—'

Somebody yelled suddenly inside the warehouse. Andrea's eyes widened as she turned her head to look, her heart suddenly filling her throat again and pounding against the roof of her mouth. Shadows pooled around the edge of the warehouse door; she could hardly see inside, couldn't see any of the men who'd carried the crate inside, but it had definitely come from somewhere in there.

'Hold this for a second,' she said, thrusting the staff back into Rachel's arms and jogging toward the warehouse entrance. She crossed the threshold and looked left and right, scanning the spaces between huge, steel racks and mountains of boxes until she saw them.

Karl and his men all stood beside the crate, which had been heaved off the low-loader and stood in a dark corner of the warehouse, the dull amber glow of a naked bulb above them seeping steadily into the veins of every wooden panel, absorbed by the box itself.

The foreman turned as she neared them, marching purposefully toward the crate. He smiled sheepishly.

'What happened?' Andrea said. 'Is everyone all right? Karl?'

'Everyone's fine,' the foreman nodded. He clapped a thick-fingered hand on the shoulder of the man standing next to him. 'Nothing to worry about. Only our Jez here losing his mind. Saw a cockroach, poor bugger.'

Jez's face was white as a sheet. He could only have been sixteen or seventeen, Andrea thought, with sallow cheeks and a blotchy birthmark in the shape of a feather running down his jawbone. 'Just a roach,' he nodded. 'You drop your guard a little when you're lifting something that heavy. Ran right past my feet. Sorry, everyone.'

Andrea nodded, keeping her eyes on the boy's face. He looked terrified, she thought, like he'd seen a ghost rather than a cockroach. Poor kid.

'All right, lads,' Karl said, clapping his hands together. 'Let's crack on and get the rest of this truck unloaded, shall we?'

He turned to leave, two of the others following him

toward the warehouse entrance. Andrea glanced up at the crate, suddenly aware that she was standing directly in its shadow. Only after a few moments had passed did she notice the presence beside her; she lowered her head.

Jez stood inches from her, his eyes on her face, his pupils dilated. His lips were parted as though he'd been about to say something.

'You all right?' Andrea said warily.

'What's in there?' Jez whispered. He looked in the direction of the others; Andrea could hear them laughing as they stepped out of the warehouse and back onto the courtyard, their voices fading into a distant murmur.

'In the box?' Andrea said carefully. 'Nothing special,' she lied. 'Just one of my new exhibits. Why?'

Jez didn't answer; he just gazed up at the box, seemingly afraid of it.

'Hey. What's the matter?'

He looked back at her. 'I didn't see no roach,' he said, his voice trembling.

She frowned. 'No? Then what?'

'We were taking the crate off the trolley,' he said, 'and it… *spoke* to me.'

Andrea cocked an eyebrow. 'Excuse me?'

'It whispered. Or… or something *in* it whispered. Right in my ear.'

'And what did it say?' Andrea said, swallowing

nervously.

For a long time, the boy was silent. And then he smiled weakly, shook his head, and said, 'Nothing. I must have imagined it. It's like I say, when you're focused on carrying or whatever, your mind sort of... runs away with itself.'

'All right, well, what did you *think* it said?'

He looked at her. Paused. 'I thought it said my name. Jeremy.'

Andrea blinked.

'But it can't have, right? There's nothing in there. Nothing alive.'

'No, of course not,' she said.

From the courtyard, somebody called for the boy. He flinched. 'Well, I better get back out there. You won't... tell anyone, will you? They'd never let me hear the end of it. And if my missus finds out, she'll think I'm going nuts.'

Andrea shook her head. 'I won't say anything.'

Jez turned to follow the others, scratching the back of his neck, and Andrea was left alone in the looming shadow of the crate. When she looked up at it, a sickly cold feeling spread down her spine.

It almost felt like it was looking back.

Chapter 2

Andrea's office was the approximate square footage of a caretaker's cupboard, but she had somehow filled it with half of the Historical Museum's library. Many of the books scattered across and around her desk were open, and where they had been closed and stacked in the corner beside a pair of tall, steel filing cabinets she had slapped post-it notes onto them to remind her to return them as soon as possible. A wire 'in' tray on her desk was lined with felt and packed with ancient coins and artefacts: a jet-black stone fertility idol lay among a small pile of forged Aztec gold; lined up neatly beside a cranky old laptop were three ancient daggers, organised by size so that her mouse cable trailed across the rusted handle of the longest, a Roman pugio with a blade carved from a single shaft of polished bone. These were the pieces that interested Dr Andrea Cain the most: the odd, the strange, sometimes the occult and mysterious. Most of the books she had open were specialised, some written by her peers, all detailing various facets of ancient history from Greco-Roman magic to Mesoamerican deities.

She stumbled into the office with red flushing her cheeks, carrying the long package awkwardly in both arms. Swinging the door closed with her butt, she headed straight for the desk and bent down to swipe her papers into a haphazard pile with her elbow. Grunting softly, she laid the package down across her desk and stood back, clapping dust off her hands. Absent-mindedly she reached for the coathook by the door and swung on her work jacket, a crisp, grey blazer to match her skirt. The cold chill that had begun to crawl beneath her skin down in the warehouse had not left her now that she'd come back upstairs. Through the wall behind her, she heard the low buzz of conversation from Dr Melvin Phillips' office; from further away, she could hear the constant tramp of footsteps and the chatter of kids and families from the museum itself. She was deep in the bowels of the building, in a modern-ish wing that had been slapped onto the centuries-old building in the late seventies, and for some reason soundproofing had never once been considered during construction.

Sighing, she moved to the desk and began to unwrap the parcel.

It was about seven feet long, barely a couple of inches in diameter, save for the very top where the packaging bulged crudely around an irregular kind of growth. The tape was too tight for her to pick at with much success, as chipped and short as her fingernails were, and so she bent over the desk to grab a pair of scissors from a coffee jar packed with pens and highlighters. She grabbed her reading glasses from atop her laptop and poked them onto her nose, squinting closely as she carefully sliced through the packaging.

Laying the scissors down, she tucked her glasses into the neck of her blouse and stood straight, looking down at the thing across her desk. The cellophane lay open around it, so that the impression was almost one of a plant's petals peeling open with the heat. The thing itself was like nothing she had ever seen.

It was beautiful.

The artefact was clearly ceremonial, but in shape and length it looked more like a warrior's spear than the staff of a priest. The shaft was a long, inch-thick pole of matte black metal, so absolute in its darkness that it looked like obsidian; like she could jam her fingers into that black and never get them back. It had rusted in patches, one about halfway up where she supposed it had been handled the most, and one near the base which spread into a mottled crust of red and then split the pole into a ruptured mess of coppery-gold right at the end. Thin rings of gold, like wedding bands, had been welded onto the shaft at irregular intervals all the way up its length; at one point, there were three of these crudely-fused bands within three or four inches; further up, a stretch of shaft about nine inches long went interrupted.

The head of the shaft was a thing of beauty, and a large part of the reason it looked so deadly. A crown of finely-carved ivory had been fused to the top of the pole with more gold, and where that bone had been cracked or damaged yet more gold had been poured into the cracks so that thin slivers shone across the skin of the thing. It was shaped like a thick, hooked arrowhead, spines jutting from it like barbed teeth. And nestled within a crook in the ivory, a green gem the size of a baby's clenched fist shone in the dim light of her office, sharp corners catching that light and throwing it back as a mass of sizzling, emerald embers. The stone itself must have been insanely valuable, Andrea thought, but in the curved palm of the ivory-headed spear it was a blazing green crown of beauty that she could barely imagine separated from its morbid mantle.

Her phone buzzed in the pocket of her blazer and she jumped, fumbling for it. Ripping her eyes from the spear, she held the device to her ear and answered. Pain shot through her knuckles and wrist as her fingers locked onto the phone; she winced. 'Dr Cain speaking, who's this?'

'Hey, Andy. Everything all right? You sound like you're in the middle of something.'

Andrea let out a breath that had hitched in her throat. 'Oh, Bruce. Hi. Sorry, I – uh, no, not in the middle of anything, sorry. Some new exhibits came in, I've just been looking through them. What's up?'

The voice on the other end of the line was thick and soft, gravelly from a smoking habit that she knew the speaker was trying desperately to give up. 'I was just checking, still on for dinner tonight?'

'Tonight?' she frowned. 'What day is it today?'

'Andy, it's—'

'Oh, god. Sorry. I didn't forget, it's just... been a long morning, sorry. Tonight, yes.'

'Tonight being?'

'A year since we started going out,' she smiled. 'Do I pass?'

'Pass what?'

'Your memory test.'

'Depends if you can remember when and where our table's booked,' Bruce said coyly, his voice crackling with static as though he were travelling through a tunnel.

Andrea's eyes fell back onto the spear. She froze. Oh, god. She couldn't.

'Just kidding,' Bruce said. 'I'm surprising you, remember?'

'Jesus, Bruce, don't *do* that to me today.' She frowned, suddenly noticing something near the head of the spear that she hadn't seen before. She moved closer

19

to the desk, tilting her head to pin the phone in the crook of her shoulder as she grabbed a pair of purple latex gloves and snapped them on. Gingerly, she gripped the spear by the shaft and rolled it over so that the vicious hook of its head was pointed upward. She squinted, looked closely. Something… she had seen it, she was certain, just a moment before…

'So I'll come pick you up after work?' Bruce said.

'Oh. Yes. Yeah, I'll see you then.'

'You sound excited.'

'I am, Bruce – sorry, I really am.' She paused for a moment, stepping back from the spear and closing her eyes. She breathed, held it. 'I am excited. Sorry, I don't mean to be dismissive.'

'You're absolutely fine,' he said. 'I'll see you later.'

'Love you.'

'Catch you after work,' Bruce said softly. The line died.

Andrea opened her eyes, gently pulling at her jacket's lapel and letting the phone slide off her shoulder and into the inside pocket. Clearing her throat, she returned to the spear.

Something…

There.

Right near the bony head of the thing, clear as day. So plain that she couldn't believe she hadn't spotted it before.

'Oh,' she said, her voice suddenly very weak.

***

The museum closed at five o'clock that evening. The magnificent building was washed in the amber glow of a series of powerful streetlamps, the locked front doors standing sentry at the top of a wide, smooth stone staircase. The ancient pillars of the building were pocked and scarred with age, but no less spectacular than they had been hundreds of years ago; in fact to some it might have been even more beautiful like this – shadows dribbling through every crack, pale stone illuminated in shades of mellow gold and moonlight – than in the day. Either side of the door, a gently billowing banner advertised the newest exhibition. *Mysteries of the Ancient World* was emblazoned on each in bright, blazing white, and photographs of Ancient Mayan weaponry and Roman skulls had been superimposed on a background of eerily glowing question marks.

The warehouse and courtyard were floodlit, a skeleton crew mostly busy forklifting the last delivery of the day into storage. In a far corner of the warehouse, Wham! played softly on an old workman's radio.

Jez stood hunched over a makeshift workbench in a nook beside the warehouse doors, humming to himself. Working by the light of the dim bulb above him – the floodlights outside didn't reach him here – he pored carefully over a stack of paperwork. His mind was elsewhere. His shift was ending at seven; Lyssa had promised to cook chilli. She had suggested they go out to dinner, but he knew he'd be exhausted – and besides, he had plans to take her out at the weekend. Big plans.

He smiled a little, scratching his head. The paperwork was a mess, and his skull felt like it was melting. Maybe he'd head up into the staff wing of the museum, run to the toilet quickly. He didn't need to go, but the walk through the bright corridors upstairs usually did a good job of waking him up.

Yawning, Jez turned to glance toward the lift. Briefly, his eyes passed over the crate in the corner of the warehouse.

It stood taller than any of the boxes and cartons around it, casting a huge, square shadow onto the concrete floor. The lights flickered for a moment, causing him to jump and look away again. When he looked back, the lights had come back on – dimmer now, weakened by the temporary surge of power – and the eight-foot crate was little more than a silhouette. A looming, great slab of a silhouette. He shuddered.

'Storage Three,' he murmured, turning back to the paperwork. It would be stupid to try and move the crate by himself, but maybe he could wrestle a couple of the other guys from the forklift and get them to help him out with it. He'd just feel... more *comfortable*, he thought, if it was in one of the other hangars.

If it wasn't there, watching him.

'You're being dumb,' he said, shaking his head. He stepped back from the paperwork and squeezed his eyes shut, pinching the bridge of his nose with two fingers. He could feel a migraine coming on. Had he actually booked the table for Saturday night? He had the ring in his pocket; he could feel the bulge of the little case against his hip. He'd arranged to pick up the flowers on Saturday afternoon, he was sure. And the restaurant…

Oh, he couldn't think about it now. He was tired, and every thought felt like it was rolling languidly down a tar-covered slide in his head – if he leant forward, they'd roll into his eyes and punch them out of their sockets, and if he tipped it back, they'd start rolling toward the base of his skull; but if he balanced his head just right…

Something rattled loudly behind him.

Jez wheeled around, eyes snapping open wide. 'Hello?' he called.

Nothing.

As he turned back to his crude desk, his eyes fell onto the crate again. He paused, staring at the thing, squinting into the dark as if he might be able to pick out some new detail in the wood.

'Stop it,' he scolded himself, tearing his eyes away. Outside, he heard the echoing beep of the forklift reversing into one of the smaller storage hangars.

Laughter as two of the day crew prepared to leave for the evening.

Jez glanced at his wristwatch. Perhaps he could clock out early; get back to Lyssa and the dog, forget about today. He'd text her before he left and ask her if she'd mind cooking a little sooner than she'd planned, then they could have an early night.

'Sounds like a plan,' he muttered, folding the paperwork into a small drawer at the back of his workbench. His head was pounding. Pounding...

Again, something rattled deep in the warehouse. Jez wheeled back, looking in the direction of the sound, somewhat unsurprised that it was coming from somewhere near the crate.

Nothing moved. Perhaps there was a rat or a mouse somewhere in the rafters, or maybe it was one of the guys trying to spook him. Well, they'd have a damn hard time, he thought, narrowing his eyes at the crate. To himself, he murmured, 'Jez don't spook for *nothin*'.'

A full minute passed, and nothing. No rattling, no mice, no nothing.

'All right, that's quite enough for one day,' he grunted, turning back to the desk and fumbling in his jeans for his car keys. His knuckles rolled over the velvet case of the ring in his pocket and he smiled weakly. Saturday night, that was when it all changed. For better or worse, right? 'Let's get out of here, shall we?'

Behind him, the crate trembled.

Jez froze. He could see it in the corner of his eye: shadows dripped slowly down the crate as it shook on its feet, and there was that rattling again. Something moving inside the box, moving animatedly enough that the whole thing shuddered. Slowly, he turned his head.

It stopped the moment he laid his eyes on it, as though the thing inside had seen him. But then, as if it had decided that was exactly what it wanted, the crate started to shake again.

'Oh my god,' Jez whispered.

With a final thump, the crate stood still.

'Rats,' he said aloud. 'Fuckin' rats, I'll bet.'

Darkness swelled around him. Overhead, the lights had started flickering again. Bending down, he reached into a rack beneath the workbench and pulled free a yellow-handled crowbar, a thick flat shaft of iron curved into a blunt, forked tongue. He moved purposefully toward the crate, half-expecting it to fall open at any moment and let loose a flood of hundreds and thousands of skittering, scratching rats. He swallowed.

The crate trembled again. Now that he was closer he could hear the thumping from inside much more clearly. It didn't just sound like rats, it sounded... bigger. Bigger and angrier.

'Right,' Jez growled, his voice on the edge of

breaking. He tensed his shoulders, gripping the crowbar in one hand and flexing his knuckles. Hoping he appeared braver than he felt. 'If there's some bastard in there playing silly buggers with me, you'd better say something before I break this open!'

The thumping continued. Now it sounded more like knocking; Christ, perhaps someone was *trapped* in there, and suffocating, desperate to get out…

'Hold on!' Jez grunted, jamming the crowbar into the slats and preparing to yank off the front face of the crate. The knocking was a frantic hammering now, echoing in his ears and all around him, drowning out the pounding of blood in his head. 'Just a—'

The crate swung open before he could twist and he yelped as a great heavy pane of wood fell forward, twisting his arm back. The crowbar fell out of his hand and skittered across the floor; he clutched his wrist, staggering away from the crate.

He stood panting, staring into the darkness inside the crate. Dim light glanced off flecks of what must have been some kind of reflective stone, scattering points of white across the shadowy contents of the box.

Two of the white points of light winked out. He froze. The thumping had stopped; an awful, musty smell rose from the crate, accompanied by something else, something… fresher.

The two white points reappeared, closer, and now Jez saw that they were eyes.

His breath hitched in his throat and he backed away, desperately shaking his head. 'No,' he moaned, 'no, no, no…'

The darkness screeched like a banshee, and a terrible shape lurched forward from within the crate and thrust its fingers toward him.

Chapter 3

Bruce came to pick Andrea up from the museum a little after five. The front doors were locked, but a buzzer beside the single glass door around the side of the main building let him call her directly, and she came down into the alleyway shortly after. Bruce was dressed in his work clothes: a crisp, blue suit and tie and polished brown shoes. His beard was thick and black but trimmed neatly to his jaw, and his hair was combed smartly. His eyes were a piercing, cold blue.

'Hello, gorgeous,' Bruce said softly as she stepped outside, letting the door fall closed behind her. The early evening was cool, a bank of clouds above the building only just beginning to tinge with gold. 'You ready?'

She nodded excitedly, looping a thick, red scarf around her neck. 'Where are we going, then?' she said, taking his hand and heading quickly down the alley. His Lexus would be parked where it usually was, on the kerb down Williams Street. The inside of the car always smelled like walnuts.

'I thought we'd go back to Comida Caliente,' Bruce said, his grip on her hand tight and formal. 'That was good the last time.'

He had been smoking, she thought: the muscles of his neck were strained and his temple throbbed. 'That would be nice,' she said. 'Then back to mine after? We can put the telly on for a bit, have some wine.'

He smiled thinly. 'We'll see.'

They turned onto Williams Street and Bruce let go of her hand, reaching inside a thick, brown overcoat for his car keys.

Andrea froze as a blood-curdling shriek bounced off the walls around them. Her head snapped around and she looked back toward the museum. The sound was awful, animalistic – it only lasted for a moment, but it rang loudly in her ears even after it had faded. 'What was that?' she whispered.

Bruce had moved to the car, and barely looked up. 'Probably an owl,' he said absent-mindedly. 'Nothing to worry about, Andy.'

'It was coming from the museum—'

'Just an owl,' Bruce repeated curtly. 'Ready?'

Andrea hesitated, her eyes on the roof of the museum, a slanting pane of old lime above the other buildings. She swallowed. 'Yeah, ready,' she said, and she turned and stepped toward the car.

The restaurant was nice enough, and only a very short drive from the museum; they had been three or four times, and Andrea thought it was the perfect blend of affordable food and fancy atmosphere. The walls were bright yellow and an assortment of Spanish instruments and paintings cluttered them. Diners sat in front of the huge glass windows and chattered quietly. Andrea ordered the paella.

'So how was work?' she asked, sipping slowly on a small glass of red wine.

'Fine,' Bruce shrugged. He worked his jaw anxiously as he spoke. 'Not much to report, sadly. Same old, you know? Though I did score a new client for Reynolds, should be worth a good fifty grand a year.'

'Oh? That's great, Bruce. I told you he'd be thrilled he gave you that promotion. You deserved it.'

Bruce nodded, his eyes faraway as though he hadn't heard her. 'And a good chunk of bonus for me, of course.'

'Very nice,' Andrea smiled. 'A productive day, then.'

A few moments passed in silence, the low thrum of conversation around them dipping and swelling as the warm glow of dozens of amber filaments spread over the tablecloth. Eventually, Bruce said, 'How was yours?'

'Hmm?' Andrea said, drawing her attention back to the table. She had been watching the window across from them as a pair of silhouetted drunkards fought half-heartedly in the square. At the far edge of her vision, the museum building was a wide, pointed shadow in the fading dusk light.

'Your day. How was it?'

'Oh, very exciting,' Andrea said, leaning forward. 'I finally had that exhibit delivered. You know – the one I was telling you about? The last piece for the exhibition. I'm going to open it up tomorrow and see what I can dig up before it goes on display next week. I'll have to send you some photographs so you can see—'

She paused and leant back again as the waitress arrived with their food. Apologising for interrupting their conversation, the narrow Spanish woman laid down Andrea's paella and a platter of ribs for Bruce. 'Can I fetch you anything else?'

'I think I'm all right, thank you,' Andrea said. 'Anything for you, Bruce?'

'Fine, thanks,' he said. The waitress nodded and left them.

'Anyway,' Andrea said as she dug into the rice, her fingers throbbing as they curled awkwardly around the fork. The hearty smell of prawns and paprika wafted into her nose. 'I hope you can come to the exhibit when it opens. I'd love to see what you think.'

'Mm,' Bruce said absently, sucking meat off a curved, grey bone and jabbing a sticky hand into the napkin on his lap.

'Do you think you'll be able to leave work early and come see?' Andrea said. 'I sent you the date, I don't know if you've asked yet—'

'I can take whatever time I need, Andy, Reynolds won't mind.'

'So you'll come?' Andrea beamed.

Bruce frowned up at her. 'Come to what?'

Andrea's face fell. 'My exhibition. Next Friday, I was just talking about it.'

'Oh. Yeah, definitely.'

Andrea took another sip of wine, glancing away.

Still frowning, Bruce said, 'I think this is raw, you know.' Before Andrea could say anything, or even look at his plate, he had stuck up a hand. Impatiently he clicked his fingers. 'Waitress!'

Andrea cringed. The young woman returned quickly to their table and asked if everything was okay.

'I think you ought to tell me,' Bruce said, gesturing at his plate. 'Does this look okay to you?'

'Bruce!' Andrea hissed, shocked.

'I'm just asking the lady if she'd eat this,' Bruce said calmly. Looking up, he said, 'Would you?'

'I... I'm sorry, sir, if there's a problem with your meal I can—'

'I'd like you to try a little,' Bruce said, pushing the plate toward her.

'Bruce, that's enough,' Andrea said. Turning to the waitress: 'I'm so sorry. Everything's fine.'

'No, it isn't,' Bruce said. 'I'd like to speak to the chef, please.'

'Certainly,' the waitress nodded quickly. 'I'll – I'll just run and fetch him for you, sir.'

'Good.'

She left.

Andrea seethed.

'Lord, whatever are you looking at me like that for?' Bruce muttered, shaking his head and snatching the plate back. 'You know we'll get a little off the bill for this.'

'Oh, your bonus wouldn't have covered it otherwise?' Andrea said.

'I'm sorry?' Bruce cocked an eyebrow, looking at her now as though seeing her for the first time since they'd sat down. He reached up and straightened his tie, working his jaw anxiously. 'There's no need to be upset with *me*, you know. Jesus, what's taking them so long?'

'Is it really raw, Bruce?'

'What?'

'The ribs. Are they raw, or not?'

'Well, they're a little—'

'Let me see,' she said, leaning across for his plate.

34

Quickly she dug her fork into the slab of seared meat and pulled a hunk off the bone. 'God, Bruce, it's fine.'

'You don't see the pink in there?'

'No,' she said flatly, sliding the plate back to him, 'and neither do you. Now, when the chef comes out here, you're going to tell him you made a mistake, and when the waitress comes back to our table – god, if she *dares* come back to our table after that outburst – you're going to apologise to her. And when we leave tonight, you're going to leave a nice tip. All right?'

'Well, we shan't come here again,' Bruce grumbled.

'I shall,' Andrea said.

Bruce left the restaurant before their dessert had arrived, telling her he needed some air. She watched him through the window as she ate her ice cream, fuming quietly between each mouthful. When it appeared he wasn't coming back, she started to eat his too, and after waiting for another ten minutes she raised her hand for the bill.

With his back to the glass, Bruce stood almost entirely still for most of that time, but occasionally his hand would move to his face and, shortly after, a puff of grey smoke would blossom in front of him. Andrea wondered if he'd given up trying to hide it, or if he'd simply forgotten she was there.

When she had paid, she stood, pulled on her coat, and tucked a twenty-pound note under her empty wine glass. Quickly draining the rest of Bruce's drink, she nodded an apologetic goodbye to the waitress who'd served them and headed outside.

It was cold outside, the only real light in the square coming from the glass wall behind her. Narrow buildings loomed all around, the shopping district to the right all shut up and the market stalls between them covered in tarp. A row of orange streetlights along the distant face of the museum building looked like a string of fairy lights. She shivered.

'Will you take me home, please?' she said as she stepped out of the door.

Bruce hastily dropped his cigarette to the floor and stamped it out.

'Oh, don't bother,' Andrea said.

Bruce looked at her. His expression had softened, but he was still pouting like a child.

'Will you take me home?' she repeated.

'Yeah,' he said quietly. 'Yeah, of course. Listen, Andy—'

'Save it. Let's go.'

She turned and started walking to the car. Bruce hurried to catch up, fumbling for his keys. 'Andy, I'm sorry, really. I didn't mean to embarrass you.'

'It's fine. Don't worry,' she said, pulling open the door.

'Andy, I mean it… I'm sorry. Really. What… what are you looking at?'

Andrea's eyes had moved past his face to the museum across the town square. It was difficult to discern in the dark, but the streetlamps threw waves of muddy amber up the pillars and onto the roof, one or two of them flickering so that it almost looked like firelight. The moon hung fat and bloated in a bank of wispy black cloud behind the building, casting its own desperate blue onto the limestone ridge that crowned the museum, a flat banner of stone that dipped down into a wide, metal-plated gutter before the roof begun to slant up.

There were people up there. A dozen shadows, so distant that she almost thought she might be imagining them. But no – lined up along the roof, their exact shapes indiscernible as though they were wearing thick robes – ten or twelve figures stood at regular intervals, looking down on the square from above.

'What is it?' Bruce said, turning to follow the direction of her gaze. His head swung in front of hers for a moment.

When his body lilted back again, the people on the roof had gone.

Chapter 4

The space the creature had found itself in was dark and narrow, shooting vertically up through the neck of the building. It clung to ruts in the wall with crooked fingers that each held an unnatural amount of strength, though they were little more than crumbling bone. Its whole body was an assault against the physical laws that should have pulled it apart; gauze that should have decayed centuries ago was fused to an ancient crust that, though dusty and flaking, did not rot as it should have.

It was hungry. Flashes of gold hung around its neck and wrists, heavy shards of a memory that burned in the long-shrunken husk of its empty chest. Its body was spindly and felt sore and empty, despite the blood drooling from its open, gurning maw. Rags shot through with bites and scratches coiled around its shoulders and hips and flailed in the empty dark of the shaft beneath it.

Hungry, but patient. It had waited for thousands of

years. And the agony it felt now, the rage, was nothing.

But it would grow.

Andrea went straight down to the warehouse the next morning to begin work on the contents of the crate. The mystery of the staff in her office had stumped her temporarily; it was something she'd have to discuss with the curator, but that could wait. She had taken two benzodiazepines the night before and slept peacefully for most of the night, and felt rejuvenated and eager this morning.

She hadn't heard from Bruce since he'd dropped her at her apartment.

'Morning, Karl,' she said cheerfully as she came into the warehouse, taking a sip from her Starbucks and dropping a tray of four more paper cups onto his workbench. The foreman looked up, smiling tightly and nodding his thanks for the coffees.

'Appreciate it,' he said absently, turning back to his paperwork. Behind them, two men in hi-viz vests were guiding a delivery lorry backward through the tall iron gates of the courtyard.

'Everything all right?'

Karl nodded, frowning down at his desk. 'Yeah, fine, sorry. We're short a guy today, is all. Lots to get through without him.'

Andrea glanced toward the back of the warehouse

and saw that the space where the crate had been was empty. 'Off sick?' she asked flatly. She took another sip, keeping her eyes pinned on that space. The space there was dark, the floor swallowed by the shadows of tall shelves and mountains of boxes.

'I imagine so. Or hungover.'

She turned her attention back to the foreman. 'Didn't call in?'

'Not yet,' Karl said, wrapping his hand around one of the coffee cups and taking a long drink. He looked exhausted, and Andrea noticed for the first time that his hair was starting to thin. 'You know, it's not like that Jez to do this. He's only been off a couple of times in the last year, and he gave me plenty of notice.'

'Odd, then.'

'Suppose so. Still, never mind. We'll manage without him, I guess. He's just in for a bit of a bollocking when he does decide to show up.'

'Well, thank you for getting my crate moved anyway,' Andrea said, nodding toward the empty space. 'I'll find it in Storage Three, will I?'

Karl paused, looked up. 'Ah,' he said. 'I'd forgotten about that. Something happened.'

Andrea's heart skipped a beat. 'What?'

The foreman looked her in the eyes, gripping the edge of his workbench with white knuckles. Seemed to swallow, as though nervous.

'Karl, what happened to my crate?'

He smiled weakly. 'You might want to go see the boss on that one.'

'The boss' was Dr Irene Curran, the chief curator of the Historical Museum and published author of more books and papers on Anglo-Saxon Britain than Andrea could count. She was also what Andrea would have called – in the most diplomatic way possible – an enormous and particularly sore pain in the arsehole. A woman of fifty-eight who had spent about three quarters of those years locked in her office in the staff wing of the museum, she was hard-nosed, arrogant and bullish. And annoyingly beautiful, Andrea had always thought.

She stopped outside Curran's office and flexed both of her hands, the dull throb of her arthritis pulsing from the pads of her numb fingers to her wrists and back again. Her knuckles felt stiff and useless, and the swelling of her wrists ached gently into the soft flesh of the heels of her hands. She refused to look down, knowing that her hands would be warm and alarmingly red. Quickly she stretched her fingers as far as she could and curled them back in until they locked. Drawing in a deep breath, she approached the door and went to knock with the back of her hand—

And stopped. Inside, she could hear voices. Melvin Phillips was in there, already arguing with the curator about something. Well, damn it, she would just have to hurry them along.

She knocked, pressing open the door with her free hand before Curran could call out an answer.

'Morning,' she said, nodding vaguely in the direction of the large, oak desk in the centre of the room. 'Morning, Mel.'

'You too?' Curran said. 'Good god, what have I done now?'

The office was large and the space mostly empty, save for a few high shelves at the back of the room and a fat filing cabinet beside the door. An antique clock on the wall churned its hands loudly with a repetitive *bok—bok--bok*. Behind the desk, Dr Curran sat in a high-backed office chair with one hand on her hip and a ballpoint pen in the other, her full, red hair pinned back from a stern face and her bottle-green blouse adorned with a pair of shining blue scarab brooches. A thick grey overcoat was folded over the back of the chair.

'What are you in for?' Andrea said, turning to Phillips. He stood beside her, hands in his pockets, his head completely bald save for two waxed strips of grey hair above his ears. He was plump, dressed in a sharp grey suit and a poorly-fitting mustard yellow waistcoat. Andrea always thought he looked like he belonged in a nineties movie – and smelled like it too; she could almost taste the Old Spice wafting off him.

Still, the old man was pleasant enough, and a decent friend.

'Ms Curran has decided to downsize the Boudica exhibit,' Phillips said sourly, deliberately evading the word 'doctor'. He spoke like he was in a nineties movie, too, his voice reminding Andrea of an English impressionist's version of Tom Hanks in *You've Got Mail*. He gave Curran a pointed look. 'She's under the impression that museum visitors are far less interested in the Romans than we thought, and believes that thirty per cent of the space allocated to my showcase would be better used to display a range of significantly more *modern* pieces.'

Andrea's heart sunk into her stomach. 'Is that what's happened to my crate? You've downsized my *Mysteries* exhibit? Irene, don't tell me you sent it back.'

'What?' Curran frowned. 'Your crate?'

'The crate in the warehouse,' Andrea said. 'My sarc—'

'Oh! Of course,' Curran said, snapping her fingers excitedly. 'That's what I meant to talk to you about! Another half hour, Dr Cain, and I'd have been in your office. Your crate's perfectly safe – in fact, it's already been unpacked, and the contents are in their place in the exhibition hall.'

Andrea stared.

'I thought I'd help you to get the exhibition

together, what with the new opening date. I didn't want you to think I'd ask you to do *everything* so much faster than originally planned.'

'Faster than – Irene, what's going on?'

Dr Melvin Phillips tucked his hands into his pockets, his cheeks flushed with anger.

'I did send you an e-mail,' Curran said, suddenly serious, her face pinched. 'Haven't you seen it?'

'When did you send it?'

'Oh – six, seven-ish, last night?'

'Then no, I haven't,' Andrea said dully. 'My exhibition wasn't scheduled to open until next week, Irene. I'd hoped to study the contents of that crate a little before putting them on display.'

'Well, I—'

'When is it opening?' Andrea said.

'Now, you mustn't—'

'When, Irene?'

Irene paused. 'Thursday,' she said.

'You're not serious. The day after tomorrow?'

'Now listen, Dr Cain. I have to consider the financial merit of every exhibition, every display, and – I'll be frank with you – we cannot continue to haemorrhage money every day that such a large section of the building is closed to visitors. You have today and tomorrow to finalise the displays, and on Thursday we open *Mysteries of the Ancient World* to the public. And you'—she turned to Phillips—'will make the best of the space you have, and respect my decision, which I can assure you has been made for the good of the museum as a whole. And, by extension, both of your jobs. Understood?'

A pregnant silence hung between them for a moment, broken only when Phillips grumbled, 'Understood.'

'And you?' Curran said, turning her face sharply toward Andrea. Two days, Andrea. Hardly any less than we'd planned. And you can study your artefacts after hours, when the museum is empty.'

'Understood,' Andrea said through gritted teeth, '*Ms* Curran.'

'Christ,' Andrea said in the corridor. 'What the hell is with her?'

Phillips shook his head. 'I've almost given up now,' he said, as they turned and started walking toward his office. 'I'm getting too old for it, Andy. I argue it every time she makes a decision like this, but… well, I'm tired. There's no sense screaming at a brick wall. I've just… got nothing left in me, you know?'

Andrea nudged him gently in the ribs with her elbow. 'You're not old. You've got plenty left in you. You're just scared of her.'

'That is true,' he smiled, but there was a sadness to the smile that told Andrea not to push him any further.

'I'll be honest, I knew this was coming. Curran's been looking at figures for the last couple of weeks, and you know once there are numbers on a page she forgets what they mean – or *who* they mean.'

'Is that why you've had Rachel working down in the warehouse?'

'I thought I'd try and nudge her into another area while the Boudica exhibit was under review. I had a feeling Curran would rather sever another pair of hands than put them to work elsewhere.'

'Makes sense. I think you should talk to her, though.'

'Who, the Iron Curator?' Phillips said as they reached the door to his office. He put his hand on the knob and shook his head. 'No chance. Haven't you been listening?'

'No, dummy, Rachel. She thinks you just didn't want her around.'

'I see. I'll catch her this morning,' Phillips said. 'You heading to your office? If you're in I'll bring you some lunch in a bit.'

'No, I'll head into the museum,' Andrea said. 'Thank you, though. I'd better get this exhibition finished before she pulls it forward to this afternoon.'

Chapter 5

The museum was busy, despite Curran's concerns, and Dr Andrea Cain practically had to fight her way through the Hall of Pleistocene Mammals just to get to the lobby.

The buzz of chatter in the grand, marble entrance hall buffeted her body like a wave as she made her way past the front desk. The acoustics carried every whispered facet of conversation, every childish hiss of excitement, every cough and sniff and footstep, up to the very top of the high, arched roof and dispersed them again; families and couples milled aimlessly between archways that led to the stuffed animals in one hall, to the Ancient Egyptians in another, to the gallery and the Hall of Victorian Industrialisation in the other direction – and to a grand, curving staircase of marble and stone that swept up the walls in a vast circular swathe.

She hurried up, apologising repeatedly as she nudged her way through the sporadic crowd. *Mysteries of the Ancient World* had been set up in Exhibition Hall 16 and she passed dozens of displays and slowly-shuffling groups of people on her way up. The halls and corridors were lit softly and lined regularly with polished glass cases and cabinets, and where the stone walls were inlaid with huge, arched windows, blooms of condensation had gathered on the panes and now seeped gently down toward each sill.

'Excuse me,' she said as she reached the door to her exhibition; it was locked, but a couple had paused just outside the door to discuss their plans for lunch. The two men stepped aside politely as Andrea reached into her jacket and she smiled her thanks, pressing her key-card to the lock and buzzing the door open.

Inside, she pressed her back to the door and closed her eyes. Her hands throbbed, but the pain was almost entirely overridden by the flares of anxiety that clouded her skull. She tried desperately to breathe, so badly shaken that her chest and lungs felt numb. She counted slowly. The room before her was quiet, and the faint murmur of voices from the corridor behind her somewhat comforting. Ten. Eleven.

She opened her eyes, drawing in a last long breath and letting it out over the next few seconds.

Calm.

Display cases and stands filled the large exhibition hall, spread apart so that the walkways and spaces between each were wide and accessible. Curran had

50

suggested laying out standing partitions from one end of the hall to the other, guiding visitors between the various exhibits, but Andrea had decided rather quickly that she'd rather people were allowed to follow their own course round the space. The exhibition was largely finished, with only a few stands around the walls empty or half-decorated. She would have liked to spend some time arranging everything so that it was exactly how she'd imagined when she'd first planned the space; there wouldn't be time enough now.

Beside many of the displays, thin pedestals had been stood and printed so that small, square plaques denoted the names and details of each exhibit. The individual items were protected behind glass screens and laid on plush velvet cushions in bottle-green and red, many of them still covered with cut-to-size sheets of cloth. Dust particles hung in the air and shifted as Andrea moved to the middle of the hall. Tall, multi-paned windows in black iron frames threw squares of mellow gold onto the floor and the wide stone walls, where a series of paintings and carvings had been hung in identical black frames. This was a room of centuries-old secrets, of occult paraphernalia and unknown artefacts. This was her proudest achievement.

She thought about calling Bruce, telling him that she was sorry for last night. What was the point? She'd only have to tell him that she'd likely be spending the next two nights at the museum. Certainly the next two evenings.

It could wait.

For now…

She stood before the thing in the centre of the hall, her thoughts finally calm and fluid, the stiffness of her lower arms forgotten; they hung by her sides limply, her fingers curled into loose hooks.

It was covered with a sheet, dust skitting off of folds in the thick, white material. It took up a huge amount of space, erected on a wide, black felt-covered dais with a good four feet of empty space around it on every side. Brass stanchions stood pompously around the display, a ring of plush red ropes connecting the top of each one and encircling it. Cautiously Andrea stepped forward, lifting one of the ropes to duck inside. She reached for the cover and, almost ceremonially, yanked it away.

The display was unsheathed with a *whoomph* and the blanket fell aside, crumpling onto the floor. Beneath it, a massive glass case lay on the dais, its end tilted upward so that the thing inside could be viewed from a little farther away – not too far, though; Andrea wanted people to get close.

Inside the case was a sarcophagus.

She marvelled through the polished glass at the thing beneath, resting on a bed of flocked red velvet. The sarcophagus was ancient, thousands of years old, and many of the markings carved into the stone were faded or wiped from its surface completely, so that from afar it might have resembled little more than a smooth slab of rock. The edges had been cut with extraordinarily primitive tools, but the detail of the surviving etchings was incredible. The sheer size of the great stone coffin suggested the importance of whoever was inside, as well as a series of sharp, green gemstones which had been inlaid around the edge of the thing. Many had fallen away or been blunted so harshly that they were barely visible, but some remained and glittered a piercing emerald in the fluorescent light of the exhibition hall.

Andrea leaned forward, almost laying her fingers on the glass. Her hand hovered above it and she traced lines and patterns as she saw them in the stone, stopping when she reached a point a little over midway up the sarcophagus. Here the rock had been carved to resemble a pair of folded arms, the fingers splayed into clawed wings of granite. Above them, a stony skull surged violently out of the rock, its mouth ripped open, the lower jaw crumbled away. Its eyes were frantic with terror, sunken sockets in a bald, grey head. The details had been immaculate, once: hard veins bulged in its throat and every tooth was sharpened, the tongue that pressed against them forked like a demon's and sprayed with white dust.

Andrea frowned as she looked down and saw that the edge of the sarcophagus was scratched. There was a thin, black space between lid and base and around this, there were chunks of rock missing, flecks of dust gathered in the scars. It looked like something had clawed manically at the stone until it had dragged thick crevices into it; like something had been trying desperately to get in.

Or out, she thought, and shuddered.

And – something else – she squinted, leaning right down to look. 'What the…'

A tiny scattering of dark spots around the claw marks: a deep, glossy red spray of blood.

One of the workmen must have cut themselves when they'd lifted it in here, she thought. It couldn't be anything else, and there really wasn't much. But it was fresh; the blood had to have been spilled in the last day or so.

'Christ,' she said, shaking her head. She stood straight, tearing her eyes off the sarcophagus and stepping toward the nearest display stand. Upon it, a leather-bound book had been laid open. A facsimile; the real copy was in the archive, packaged carefully and kept away from the sun. It had been found with the staff – the one that she remembered, now, was still in her office – and the pages of the original had been bound in a cover that was much more like skin, translucent and grey and somehow marvellously preserved through thousands of years. The pages themselves had been crusty and difficult to scan and restore, but she had done it.

The book was open to a page written in an ancient language that she wouldn't even begin to understand until she'd spent months decoding and translating. But she could guess, from the image on the next page, that the subject matter of this particular passage was something twisted and unpleasant.

She turned the page and admired the painting overleaf for the hundredth time.

The colour of the scan had been enhanced and certain sections filled in as accurately as possible, but it was difficult to look at the painting and not wish one was looking at the real thing. It was spread across both pages, splashing right to the edges, with thick black lines denoting shadows and pale shapes thrown in through the windows of what looked like a great stone temple.

On the left-hand page, a trio of silhouetted figures wielded the staff. They held it between them, a great shaft of black with a spearhead of green fire and bone – struggling not with the weight of the staff itself, but with the fantastic bolt of energy that exploded from its point. The three men were naked, though their modesty had been largely salvaged by the painter. Still, the fear in the eyes of the two faces which were turned toward her was transparent and chilling.

On the other page, a fourth figure cowered in fear of the staff. The brilliant ball of energy at the top of the spear turned to a nuclear spray of green that enveloped him, shooting through his exposed ribs and open, screaming mouth. His eyes were open too, but they shone with the same green light, sparks of it erupting from his face. He was dressed in thick, brown robes – or perhaps they had been red, when this was painted – and gold decorations adorned his chest and wrists.

They were killing him. No, more than that: there was something in the way his arms were bent out, his face twisted to one side, almost mirroring the stance of the man on the other page whose face Andrea couldn't see. In fact, almost *exactly* mirroring it. As if the three men were controlling him somehow. Puppeteering him. God, what she wouldn't give to be able to understand the strange scripture of this book, to know what was happening here. But she needed time.

Her phone buzzed and she cried out softly, dragged suddenly back into the real world. Outside the exhibition hall muffled voices swept down the corridor. She fumbled for the device and answered, almost breathlessly.

'Dr Phillips,' she said. 'What's up?'

'Are you busy?'

She looked around the exhibition hall. There was plenty still to do, especially now her deadline had been pulled forward. But he knew that, and he wouldn't be calling if it wasn't necessary. 'What do you need?' she said.

'Come and find me down in the lobby,' Phillips said. 'I think I might be going mad.'

Phillips was waiting for her by the front desk, where a small queue of visitors had begun to throw themselves at the receptionist. Andrea shot her a sympathetic look before approaching the balding man. 'What's going on, then?' she said quietly.

'Ah, well,' Phillips said, removing a hand from his trouser pocket and pointing toward the front of the building. 'Why don't we go and take a look?'

Curiously she followed him across the lobby to one of the narrow windows beside the front entrance. She winced as somebody bumped her shoulder, turning to look in the young woman's direction, and briefly glanced inside the Hall of Pleistocene Mammals. She caught a glimpse of tusk, a patch of woolly fur in the shadows, a flare of soft blue lighting. Phillips hurried her impatiently to the window and nodded out through the glass.

'What d'you think they're doing?' he said seriously.

Andrea looked outside.

The square was unusually busy, small crowds of people milling aimlessly about. If she squinted, she'd be able to make out the restaurant where she and Bruce had had dinner the night before. She almost went to look – but then she stopped.

'Oh, that's odd, Mel,' she whispered.

'I certainly thought so,' Phillips said. 'What do we do?'

If she had not been looking for something out of the ordinary, she would not have spotted them. They stood entirely still, spread thinly enough apart that they blended into the crowd. But as with any surge of movement, the eye is drawn somewhat to pillars of stillness, and she counted half a dozen of them at least.

They stood fifty or sixty feet from the museum entrance, hands folded behind their backs. Each man wore a long, orange robe, plain and featureless, and they all had their hoods drawn up to cover their faces; the only details she could discern beneath those banks of shadow were the crooked points of sharp noses and thin, pressed grimaces.

'Do you think it's some kind of protest?' Phillips said. For the past few years the English Historical Museum had been in the long, drawn-out process of returning every item of its inventory that had been wrongfully acquired or stolen from indigenous peoples and rightful owners; still, some were unhappy with just how long that process was taking, and some found other reasons to be angry – some justified, others less so.

Andrea swallowed, shaking her head. 'I don't think so,' she said. 'I don't know. But they're creeping me out. Have someone from security keep an eye on them.'

Phillips nodded.

'Let me know if they do anything,' Andrea said quietly, and she turned and headed back toward the stairs. She felt a familiar chill running down her back and ignored it. She had enough to do without worrying about some weird pack of monks that had decided to make camp right outside the doors.

Still, she couldn't help but think that there was more going on out there than she cared to know.

It was late when she left the museum, and the night was thick and inky. Bruce wasn't there to pick her up, though she hadn't expected him to be. As she stepped out through the staff doors she decided to phone him quickly. There was no sense falling out over little things, she thought. He was probably busy with work too, and would have called if he'd had the time.

No answer. She left a brief message apologising and asking him to call her back and let her know he was okay, and tucked the phone back into her pocket. It was cold again and she hugged her chest as she walked.

As she rounded the front of the museum she looked up, half-expecting to see more figures on the roof like she had seen the night before. But there were none; only a small huddle of birds, silhouetted by the shifting orb of the moon behind them. She had probably imagined it. Though she wouldn't have admitted it to Phillips, he had freaked her out earlier by pointing out those strange monk-like figures, and now she was seeing them around every corner, though he had told her at closing that they had disappeared shortly after she had gone back upstairs.

'Dr Cain!' somebody called. She wheeled around, hair billowing in her face, and saw a lithe figure jogging toward her.

'Rachel?' she said, squinting into the dark as the figure came closer. 'What are you doing here late?'

'I could ask you the same,' Rachel said, catching up to her. 'Though I think Dr Phillips has already filled me in on that one. I'm sorry about your exhibition.'

'It's still opening,' Andrea smiled thinly, 'that's the main thing. Are you coming this way?'

The dark-skinned girl nodded and they began to walk together.

'So, what about you?' Andrea said. 'I'm sure you have much better things to do with your life than hang around here after hours with all us dusty relics.'

'I've been doing some research,' Rachel said. 'Phillips caught me earlier and told me about Boudica. I thought I'd look into some other areas, since I'm not needed in his department anymore. He said he'll look into transferring me a little more officially if I can find the right fit.'

'Better to move you to another floor than let you be

laid off,' Andrea agreed. 'I'm sorry, Rachel, I know it's difficult.'

'I don't suppose I could help you with anything?' Rachel said brightly. 'Just till everything's sorted.'

Andrea paused. 'You know what, I think you could,' she said. 'Feel like spending some time with me the next couple of days?'

'Perfect.'

'Fab,' Andrea said. 'I'll meet you in my office in the morning?'

Rachel nodded. 'I'll look forward to it.'

Chapter 6

Andrea barely remembered getting home, let alone crawling into bed and turning the lights off. Still, she must've, because the next morning she woke up with the sheets twisted between her legs and the purplish afterimage of an awful dream sizzling on her eyelids. She remembered flashes: the awful grinding of stone on stone as an enormous wedge of boulder was driven slowly up across her vision; the blotting out of light as the lid closed; the terrible suffocating claustrophobia of the coffin. Gritty rock against her back, something in here with her, insects crawling over her legs as she kicked madly, pushing all her weight against the lid, useless.

She shuddered, crawling out of bed and dragging hair out of her eyes. It was still dark out, but she could hear birds singing cheerfully above the apartment and figured she should probably head to work sooner rather than later. The exhibition was opening tomorrow and there was a lot left to do.

Lethargically she turned over the phone on her bedside cabinet and squinted through her lashes at the dazzling screen. Barely four in the morning, she saw, turning off the alarm on her phone with one hand while she fumbled with the bedside lamp with the other. She swore quietly at the birds and stood up. Her pyjamas were sticky with sweat; Christ, that dream must have been awful. She still felt a little claustrophobic. Her hands and feet felt awful, and as she walked into the bathroom she carried her phone with tender fingers that refused to bend much more than twenty or thirty degrees. Her knuckles felt like pebbles, knocking each other helplessly about.

For a moment she stood by the window looking out. It was a little frosty outside, cool white tips encrusted onto the grass of a neighbour's garden, icy patches covering the long, flat roof of the garages across the road. She stared vacantly into the dull halo of a single streetlight, inexplicably thinking about her childhood. Her father, the original Dr Cain – archaeology, of course – had been a tall, narrow ghost of a man, a man who had gone almost entirely grey at thirty-four and become less than a shadow of himself by forty. And Andrea's mother, a stony pillar of irony and sardonic detachedness who had turned her husband from an outgoing, accomplished scientist into a quiet, timid shell that she had, only a few years after Andrea was born, divorced.

Andrea moved away from the window, crossing the bedroom in her bare feet and stepping out into the hall. She headed into the bathroom and laid her phone on top of the radiator, only noticing when she jammed her toothbrush into her mouth that it was flashing at her. Bruce had left her a message. She listened while she brushed.

'Hey, sweetie,' he started, his voice crackling through the phone's crappy speaker, 'I just wanted to say I'm sorry for the other night. I guess I was a little carried away with everything... yeah, I'm sorry.'

Andrea winced as the toothbrush fell from her hand. Her joints were like stone; in fact her whole body ached as though she were made of granite. The haunting images of her dream hadn't yet faded – she could almost feel the bugs crawling over her feet as she hammered on the lid of the sarcophagus. Awkwardly she started brushing again. A quick shower would help her forget.

'If you want to try again, I'd love to take you out to dinner tomorrow night? Anyway, you sleep well – I'm sure you must be in bed by now, I know it's late – and hopefully I'll see you soon. Take care, Andy.'

Andrea spat and checked the time-stamp absent-mindedly: the message had been left a little after midnight. God, had he finished work that late? Or – more likely – was that just the first time all day that he'd thought about her? Momentarily she was angry, but then she thought again of her mother – how critical and dismissive she had been of Andrea's father, and how that had utterly ruined him – and she screwed the anger up into a ball and tossed it into the steadily-filling waste bin at the back of her skull.

'Ah, give him a break,' she murmured, laying the phone back down and turning to the shower. If there was one thing she never wanted to become, it was her mother.

For much of the morning Andrea and Rachel worked in silence, rearranging exhibits and polishing glass. Occasionally the older woman would send Rachel to the printer in the staff corridor to fetch a small batch of documents, and in these moments she would close her eyes and try to de-stress. Rachel was helpful, and inquisitive, and when she paused to ask a question about one of the displays Andrea was more than happy to take a quick break from polishing dust off one of the many skulls along the wall and chat with her. The skulls watched, grinning, many of them bronzed or completely blackened with age, and all with mysterious wounds and deformations. They were like a little gaggle of cruelly-gurning spectators to the last-minute chaos in the exhibition hall.

A little after eleven o'clock, the icy breeze that was

Dr Curran wafted stiffly into the hall. Her arms were folded, her eyes narrowed and scouring. Andrea caught her eye as she nodded around the room, the curator's face a mask of indifference.

'Coming along nicely,' Curran said, moving over to where Andrea had begun attaching little black-backed plaques to the stands upon which her happy little mutant skulls sat. 'You've enlisted some help, I see.'

Andrea brushed her hands on her jeans, nodding quickly. 'She's been very useful. And I really wouldn't have had the time to finish before tomorrow on my own,' she said, half-expecting the little dig to go completely unnoticed.

Curran cocked an eyebrow, her eyes still on the young girl working across the hall. Rachel had pretended not to notice her, but Andrea could tell she was listening intently to their conversation. 'Do you expect to be finished on time?'

Andrea seethed quietly. 'I couldn't honestly say,' she said curtly, 'I had a week's worth of work left to do, and now I don't have a week.'

'Look, I know you're not happy with my decision,' Curran said, finally turning to face the younger woman. 'But I hope you can at least understand my reasoning. I know you feel just as strongly about this museum's continuing wellbeing as I do.'

'Yes,' Andrea said, 'of course I do. But—'

'And if you ever want my job,' Curran said, 'you'll

have to start learning to make sacrifices when necessary. Understood?'

'I never said anything about wanting your job.'

'No, but I know you,' Curran said, almost softly. 'And I know you're capable of this, but sometimes you need a little push. Are we *understood*?'

Andrea nodded.

'Good. Crack on,' Curran said, throwing one last long, hard look in Rachel's direction before turning to leave the exhibition hall.

Andrea was gazing down through the polished, glass case around the sarcophagus when Rachel came back from her lunch break. The younger woman crossed the exhibition hall to meet her, handing her a Subway in greasy paper and setting a pair of coffee cups down on the floor. Andrea thanked her and absent-mindedly unwrapped her sandwich, turning her attention back to the sarcophagus.

'What is it?' Rachel said. 'I mean, I know what it is. Where did it come from?'

'South America,' Andrea said. She took a bite, chewed it thoughtfully. 'Phillips sent me an e-mail when they found it, thought it would be a perfect fit for *Mysteries of the Ancient World*. Truth is, it was found in an underground cache in Peru, along with a whole load of artefacts and remains, but most of those seemed to have been brought over – smuggled, most likely – from somewhere else entirely. The whole cache was mismatched, pieces from all over the world, some clearly stolen, some less obvious.'

'It's old, though.'

'Very. Older than any I've ever seen. You know, when they excavated Saqqara, they found a sarcophagus that was over three thousand years old?'

'And you think this might be older.'

'I do. And I'm sure we'll find out, in time. I'd hoped to spend some time examining it before it came up here, but now it looks like I'll have to wait till the exhibition's finished.'

'How old do *you* think it is?'

Andrea smiled. 'It could be four, five thousand years old. It could be older still. The truth is, I have no idea. We'll have to try and carbon date it, when I can get the equipment in here. When I have the time. Till then…'

'Have you seen inside?'

Andrea took another bite of her sandwich. 'This is good. Is this turkey?'

'Yeah, I think so.'

'Very nice.'

'So – the sarcophagus—'

'Opening it up would be a whole thing. This thing weighs a little over a tonne and a half, if you can believe it. The lid itself makes up for about a third of that. And the risk of breaking it, or oxidising whatever's inside…'

She thought about the strange scratch marks around the edge of the lid. The spots of blood. Her blood ran cold.

'Hopefully I'll be able to x-ray it before too long,' she said, 'and then we can see about getting the lid off. Safely. Another thing I'd hoped to do *before* it went on display.'

'And what do you think is in there?' Rachel said.

Andrea grinned. Brushing crumbs off her lapel, she turned and nodded toward the book on the nearby plinth. 'I have my theories,' she said.

Moving to the book, she pointed at one of the figures in the painting.

'This fella here,' she said with her mouth full, 'I think he was some kind of magician, or sorcerer. Or he was thought to be, at least, by *these* fellas. You see, they're attacking him – with the staff, here? And I think they killed him – or, at least… well, I'll show you.'

She turned the page, flicked through a few more until she reached another painting. Spreading the pages flat, she jabbed the image with her finger.

'There,' she said. 'You see?'

The magician from the first image looked out at them again, this time painted in portrait from mid-chest upward. He was still dressed in the ceremonial robes he'd worn before, and now Rachel could see the medallion around his neck far clearer: a disc of bright gold inlaid with delicate runes and detailed inscriptions. His bony hand was thrust up, and bangles around his wrist had been painted with the same intricate details.

He was thrusting the blade of a long, black knife up into his chin. His mouth was painted open and screaming and they could see the point of the blade poking up through his tongue and into the roof of his mouth.

His eyes were glowing green. A bright, insidious green that seemed to burn holes in the paper. They were inhuman, filled with a light the colour of death, a light that spread and torched and consumed from within.

'He killed himself?' Rachel said quietly.

'No, I don't think so. Not according to the stories in this book, anyway. Look,' she pointed at the green light in his eyes and turned back to the first painting, where she drew the pad of her finger along the length of the shining emerald beam exploding from the point of the staff. 'It's the same light here. And'—she turned the pages again, flipping back almost a dozen before landing on another illustration—'look here. The same light.'

In this painting the magician stood before a large crowd of people at the foot of what looked like a great stone monument or temple, holding the staff high above him. The same staff, bristling with the same green fire. His face was stretched into a taut grin, his free hand splayed out before him in a wide, bony claw. Every member of the crowd was lit with a shining green halo, their heads knocked back, their bodies raised inches off the muddy ground.

'He's controlling them,' Rachel said.

'Or the staff is. And I think those fellas in the first painting stole it from him, and they… well, I think they coerced him into killing himself. He looks powerful, here. Maybe he was too powerful. Whatever this light is… maybe it did more than control the living. Or maybe that was enough to condemn him.'

'As if that wasn't already too much power for one man?' Rachel said. She grinned. 'Christ, what else d'you think he was doing?'

Andrea swallowed as she thought about another of the paintings in the book, one that she'd only seen for a moment, one that hadn't left her brain since. She paused briefly, considered showing Rachel. Decided against it.

It didn't matter.

'Anyway,' she said, 'we ought to get back to it, I suppose.'

'Yes,' Rachel said, clapping her hands together. She looked around. 'God, I can't remember what I was doing. Oh – yeah, I was going to ask where you wanted me to put these, actually.'

Andrea followed her across the hall, where Rachel bent down into an open crate beneath one of the tall, arched windows. As Rachel rummaged inside the box, Andrea looked outside and down onto the square. Her heart froze cold in her chest.

'Here we are,' Rachel said. 'Do you want this with the Mayan weapons in the corner? Or… what is it?'

She followed Andrea's gaze and looked out of the window.

'Oh my god,' the younger woman said. 'What are they doing?'

Outside, a small crowd bustled across the square, nudging each other in different directions as they moved with shopping bags and thick coats. None of them seemed to notice. Andrea wondered if you would, on the ground. But from up here on the second floor it was obvious: the monk-like figures from the day before had returned. More of them this time, dressed in the same long, orange robes with their hoods pulled up. They were tall, imposing, each of them stood absolutely still with their hands hanging by their sides. And now they formed a definite line across the square, a line that curved at either end… no, not a line at all.

A circle.

They were surrounding the museum.

'What do we do?' Rachel said breathlessly.

Andrea fumbled for her phone. 'I'm going to call Phillips,' she said, 'see if he's downstairs. If he is, maybe he can get security to go out there and have a word.'

She paused for a moment as her phone screen flared up, displaying a recent text message from Dr Curran:

Some more suggestions for your exhibit. (1 Attachment: PDF)

Exhaling sharply, Andrea swiped the notification away.

'Wow, she really rides you hard, huh?' Rachel said quietly.

'Careful,' Andrea said softly, 'that's my mother.'

Before Rachel could say anything, Dr Andrea Cain had dialled Phillips and raised the phone to her ear.

'Hi, Mel. Your friends are back.'

Chapter 7

For the last four or five years, Karl Grady had taken his Wednesday lunch break religiously at exactly ten minutes past two in the afternoon. He was a decent and effortlessly approachable foreman and had always been flexible with everyone in the warehouse, but this was one thing he was absolutely rigid about. None of the packers or unloaders spoke about it, but it was silently acknowledged across the warehouse that if you had a question for Karl at five past two on a Wednesday, you saved it until he'd come back from his break.

And, of course, nobody had ever asked why, though some who had known him for many years had a pretty good idea.

It was one fifty-five now and Karl was hunched over the workbench beside the warehouse door, scribbling signatures on an eight-page document he had determinedly scrutinised for the last half hour. He had never been the kind of man who'd scrawl his name on the dotted line without knowing exactly what he was signing up for. And there were certain delivery drivers – like the PortEx driver who was currently stewing in his cab out in the courtyard – who he liked to keep waiting. This one in particular was a young man who seemed to arrive between three and four hours late every time he delivered – almost as routinely as Karl taking his lunch at the same time every day – and never offered Karl's guys a hand unloading, but sat in the cab eating a greasy baguette and watching in the wing mirror.

In fact, Karl realised, it was the same driver who'd delivered that monster crate the day before last. The little bastard had watched them unload the two-tonne thing and hadn't even opened the cab door to *ask* if they'd like another pair of hands. Well, then, he could wait a few more minutes while Karl just checked the last few details…

Quickly Karl glanced at his wristwatch. Grunted softly. Ten minutes till lunch; he couldn't keep the driver waiting too much longer, then, he supposed, or he'd be late.

'Right, you little fucker,' he murmured, quickly signing off on the last page. 'I've got places to be.'

He clapped the papers together neatly and stepped away from the workbench, heading for the door. Once the truck was in sight he raised the paperwork high in his hand, waving it so the driver could see. He caught sight of the young man's face in the wing mirror – made direct eye contact with him – and paused where he stood, hoping the driver would step out and come retrieve the papers for him. He wasn't getting any younger, and he was sure the driver would want to get going as soon as possible now he'd finished his baguette.

'Oh, come on,' Karl muttered. He lowered his arm and gritted his teeth, resigning himself to marching across the courtyard and personally delivering the paperwork to the lazy bastard. Checked his watch again: one minute past two.

Right now, Karl's husband would be stepping into Dr Masood's office in the little surgery on Eters Street, just half a mile from their apartment. Ollie would have that same nervous look on his face as he had every Wednesday afternoon; the doctor would tell him that everything was all right, that he could take his beanie off if he was comfortable, and they would begin. Right now Ollie would be answering a series of questions about his week so far, his health, his diet... and then ten minutes later, at exactly ten minutes past two, he would be taken through to the next room and they would begin his chemotherapy session.

Karl swallowed. Cursing under his breath, he stepped out of the warehouse—

Something clattered behind him.

Freezing in the doorway, Karl's grip on the

paperwork tightened suddenly; he felt the pages crumple a little in his fist. In the wing mirror of the PortEx truck, the driver frowned a little. Slowly, Karl turned his head.

The sound had come from the far end of the warehouse, where a raised concrete walkway passed the service lift and the wide glass doors to the staff staircase. Shadows shifted softly behind a high iron safety rail. Somewhere in the corner of his vision a flickering light cast odd spangles of yellow onto the edge of a metal shelf.

Keeping his eyes on the door of the service elevator, Karl turned and stalked slowly back into the warehouse. He had found himself on edge lately – in the last couple of days, in fact. Something to do with Jez. The poor kid had probably just fallen ill, but he'd been missing for two days now, and with no note or telephone call. Karl couldn't help but think that perhaps something had happened to the young man. And then there was the splinter.

'Hello?' he called, stepping into the shadows and pivoting round a stack of boxes to see the service lift better.

He hadn't told Andrea, but when Curran had asked him and the others to take that crate up into the museum, he had noticed something that hadn't been there the day before: a long sliver of wood was snapped and hanging limp from the frame, right at the edge of one of the panels, as though it had been launched off and hastily replaced. He hadn't paid too much attention to it, but it only added to his ill feeling. Somebody had been messing with the box, and, around the same time, Jez had vanished.

He looked down at his watch. Two oh-six. Four minutes until his lunch break. He would grab his sandwiches and take them out to his car, where he would sit and collect his thoughts for a few minutes. At exactly quarter past, he would telephone Ollie.

The chemo sessions were difficult, though there was a prevailing sense of vague optimism that made things easier when they spoke about it. Still, Karl knew that his husband would struggle to make it through a session without a friendly voice on the other end of the line – and, whatever his shortcomings, Karl knew that he could always provide a friendly voice. He might not be able to stop or slow down the cancer eating away at Ollie's throat and legs, but he could help him get through it. He had stopped wondering when their last day together might be, or how long Ollie had left; by the doctor's account, the man should have said his goodbyes three and a half years ago. Karl was so thankful for every spare day with him that he had almost turned to god. Then he had remembered, of course, that someone must have put those awful consuming masses in his husband's body in the first place. Still, he felt he should be thankful to *someone* up there for all the extra time they'd been given.

'Hello,' Karl called again, stepping into the corner. He was standing now where the crate had been, now a gaping square hole in the shadows that had yet to be refilled. The lights didn't quite reach him here, but if he squinted directly forward he was right in line with the service elevator. A long dark strip of shadow lay on the floor before him, a direct path through the pitch black.

Inside the service lift, something crashed. It was the sound of something heavy falling – or being thrown – and hitting a metal wall.

Two oh-eight. Two minutes. If he didn't hurry this along, Ollie would wonder what had happened. Karl couldn't bear the thought of his husband having to get through a session alone; it was bad enough that he couldn't be there in person, but not even to be able to *call…*

'All right,' he grunted, reaching into the pocket of his overalls for a small torch. Paperwork stuffed into his fist, he lifted the flashlight and illuminated the dark pathway before him.

A smear of glossy blood-red zigzagged drunkenly across the warehouse, from his feet to the ramp leading up to the elevator doors. By the time the trail reached the ramp, the flow of blood had slowed – there were only a few spattered drops of crimson on the concrete. But here – right beneath his feet – there was a great smudge of the stuff in the shape of a lazy *S*, as though whatever had dragged it across the cement had been limping on legs it didn't quite understand.

Where there were discernible footprints in the mess, they were narrow and bony – bare, with the faint imprints of toes pressed into marks that looked more like claws – and pointed inward. The heels had dragged.

Karl balked. From inside the elevator, there came another heavy *clang*. Fear gripped the man's heart like a vice and he noted the time. Two-ten exactly.

But if Jez was in there… Christ, something had happened to the poor kid and he was in there, in the lift, probably exhausted from thumping on the walls all night. Had anybody used the damn thing this morning? Evidently not, or they'd have seen him.

'Shit,' Karl muttered, stuffing the torch into his overalls and moving across the warehouse. Careful to avoid stepping in the mess, he walked deliberately and quickly to the ramp and grabbed the safety rail to haul himself up.

Seesawing between unease and impatience, Karl moved to the elevator door and listened for a moment. Nothing.

'Hello?' he called, raising a fist and hammering on the door. *Bam-bam-bam*. 'You in there, Jezzy?'

Nothing.

'All right,' he grunted, 'Sorry, Ollie, I'll only be a

second…'

He reached forward and jabbed the Call button. He waited for a moment, anxiously rapping his heel on the concrete beneath him, and then with a low grumble the doors shuddered open.

'Hell—'

His eyes widened.

'*Oh*,' he whispered.

At around the same time, Andrea's phone was buzzing in her jacket.

Bruce was immediately apologetic; he talked for a moment about the stress of his work, and said that he hadn't meant for a second to take it out on the poor waitress who'd served them – let alone on Andrea herself.

'You know, it's really not a big deal at all,' Andrea said quietly, moving to the far corner of the exhibition hall. At the other end of the room Rachel was busy erecting a flatpack display stand that seemed like something the director of Ikea might have dreamed up after a particularly long night. 'Why don't we forget all about it, yeah?'

'Yeah, I'd like that.'

'I know you're stressed, Bruce. I'm really proud of all you do at work, and I know it's not easy. But if something gets to you – if you lose your cool for a moment, like you did the other night – you know we can talk about it, yeah? We can resolve it, and make sure everything's okay. What happened didn't matter, Bruce, it's okay. I just wish you'd talked to me.'

'Yeah. That makes sense. I'm sorry, Andy.'

'Are we good, then?'

'Yeah,' he said, 'we're good. Thank you. I know it's not a big deal, but… it wasn't cool of me to go off like that. And I'm sorry. I hope we can move on, like you say, and just… have a nice time again.'

'That sounds great. Listen, I'm gonna have to—'

'What are you doing tonight?' he said suddenly. 'I'd love to take you out again, maybe go see a movie or something. What do you think?'

'Oh, Bruce, I'm really sorry, I've got to stay late at work. My exhibition's been moved to tomorrow, so everything's a little chaotic right now. But maybe tomorrow night?'

A pregnant silence hung between them, filled intermittently with the faint crackle of static.

It burst.

'What do you mean? How late?' he said, his voice blunt and dark.

Andrea faltered. 'I mean… I don't know, Irene kind of sprung this on me yesterday. I might be here a little after five, or I could honestly be here all night. I just don't know. I'm sorry, Bruce, we can always do something tomorrow night instead—'

'Look, I'm trying to do a nice thing here,' Bruce said, 'I'm trying to make up for the other night—'

'—I said it wasn't a big deal, Bruce—'

'—and you suddenly have to stay late? What is it, you avoiding me now?'

'No!' she hissed, glancing back to make sure she hadn't gotten Rachel's attention. The young girl was occupied, still struggling with the display stand. 'Of course I'm not! I told you, I have to work, that's all. I'm really sorry, I know it's—'

'And you found out about this yesterday? You couldn't have told me then?'

'What difference would it have made?' she said. 'I didn't know you wanted to see me tonight – or ever again – you weren't bloody talking to me, Bruce!'

'Oh, so it's my fault?'

The phone fell out of Andrea's hand suddenly. She winced as it hit the hard, polished floor at her feet. Paused for a moment, her eyes squeezed shut. She had been so preoccupied with the call that she hadn't noticed the growing agony in both of her hands.

Fingers curled into tight knots, she bent down and scraped her phone off the floor. Not bothering to check whether the screen had cracked, she raised it awkwardly to her ear and listened.

'—like your job is worth pulling an all-nighter, and for what? So you keep your mother happy? You know she doesn't care what you do, don't you? She'll always be disappointed in you. *Always*. And d'you know what? I'm pretty disappointed too, right now. I thought you could at least tell me something like this, especially with all I've got—'

Andrea lowered the phone, pressing it against her chest. Her ribs shuddered as tight, anxious breaths wracked her whole body. Breathe, she thought, breathe and it'll go away. She needed to get back to her office and take some of her medication. She vaguely remembered that there was something else in her office that needed tending to, as well... god, what was it?

She raised the phone to her ear again.

'—irresponsible,' Bruce was saying, 'you know, *my* job is the kind of job where you'd be asked to stay late. Are they even paying you for this? Jesus, I bet you don't even know, do—'

She hung up.

Slowly, with aching hands, she slipped the phone back into her jacket. She briefly registered that the screen had smashed; the glass was splintered and rough as it slid across the pads of her fingers.

The staff. That was it. The thing in her office that she had to deal with. She remembered looking it over, remembered freezing up as she realised what she was holding in her hands...

'Fuck off, Bruce,' she whispered, and she turned around and returned to work.

***

'What the bloody hell is taking him so long?' the driver fumed, finally crumpling the foil wrapper of his baguette into a crude ball and tossing it into the passenger footwell.

Brushing crumbs from his jeans, Reggie fumbled with his seatbelt and wrestled himself free as it snapped back past his shoulder. Grumbling loudly he shoved open the cab door and twisted his body in the seat, dropping heavily onto the concrete. He slammed the door and clapped his hands together, glancing toward the warehouse door. No sign of the foreman. Cheeky prick.

'As if I don't have enough to do,' Reggie grunted. He lumbered across the courtyard, nodding his head at a lithe-looking Black man in an EHM hi-viz. 'Oi! Where's your boss gone, eh?'

The man in the hi-viz shrugged. 'Prob'ly at his desk,' he called back, pointing vaguely toward the warehouse door.

'Fucker,' Reggie grimaced, marching for the door. He rounded it quickly, stepping over the shadowy threshold and looking round. 'You in here, boss? I've got to be in Peterborough by five, you know!'

The warehouse was empty. No sign of the foreman, or the paperwork Reggie needed to collect from him. Fucking dickhead. Didn't the prick realise how many stops he had to make before the end of the day? A minute wasted is an hour spent in regret, Reggie's dad had always said. The driver scoffed. Yeah, as if it's only ever a *minute* that gets wasted with this lot.

'Oi!' he yelled again, directing his voice into the vast concrete vagueness of the warehouse this time. 'Anyone here? I've got to *go*—'

He clocked the open service elevator across the warehouse.

The doors stuttered in their frames, two panels of bulky steel shuddering inward, inward – then crashing into something solid and shunting themselves back into the walls. He watched this happen two, three times: the doors shuddered in slowly, made it about halfway before colliding with some unseen obstacle, then crashed back with a grind and whirr of metal.

'Fuck is this?' Reggie grumbled, slogging across the warehouse toward the nearest ramp and wading up it as though through a thick gut of tar. Clambering onto the raised walkway, he looked toward the lift. 'What the...'

Karl lay in the doorway, his head snapped to one side, eyes bulging out of his skull. The left eyeball was clotted with a bloom of red, and thick tracks of glossy crimson slid out of his mouth. His chest was ripped open. As Reggie watched dumbly, the doors shuddered inward, slowly bumped into Karl's shoulders, and shunted away again. Karl's body twitched.

He was dead.

'Jesus fucking Christ,' Reggie whispered, 'Oi, mate, are you—'

There was a high-pitched shrieking sound and a dark shape slithered forward, knotting its fists into Karl's shoulders. Before Reggie could register the shape it withdrew into the elevator, yanking the wide-eyed corpse with it, and Karl was gone.

'Hey!' Reggie yelled, rushing forward on instinct as something crashed inside the lift. 'Hey, you, put him down! Put him—'

He wheeled around the open lift door and froze.

The elevator was empty. The walls were splashed with blood, and there was a dent in one as though something had been slammed into it. But the thing had disappeared, and Karl's body with it. There was nothing there. Unless…

Slowly, Reggie looked up.

A great black hole had opened in the ceiling where a hatch had been forcefully removed, the edges ragged and mangled.

Looking up through the hole, Reggie saw the elevator shaft screaming up through the building: a wide, square tunnel of grey and black, rutted with ladders and pulleys that glinted in the light of a series of flickering fluorescent bulbs running up one wall. Shadows oozed over metal rungs and trickled down thick, steel cables, and right at the top the dark was so complete that the shaft could have gone up forever.

Reggie watched as a nimble, scrawny thing skittered up the walls, dragging something limp and bloody behind it. It was strong, climbing with one hand and a pair of slender, sinewy legs. Its skin was grey and decayed, its body covered in scraps of red cloth; it was almost human, but humans couldn't climb like that, not with so much weight in one fist, not so fast—

The thing paused, halfway up the shaft, as though it had smelled something.

It looked down, and its eyes locked onto the man cowering in the elevator beneath it, and Reggie saw that it was grinning, the entire lower half of its face carved into a broken, chewed-up mess of a smile. The thing's eyes lit up like silver coins and it screeched, and the awful sound echoed down the lift shaft like the howl of a banshee.

Chapter 8

Dr Andrea Cain was polishing the glass encasing the ancient sarcophagus when somebody knocked on the door of the exhibition hall. She looked up as it opened; a stocky figure in dull grey overalls peered in, evidently surprised to see that she and Rachel were still there.

'Evening, Darren,' Andrea said, straightening up and wincing as her knees creaked. Her hands throbbed painfully and she dropped her cloth onto the glass, worried that she might lose her grip on it suddenly otherwise. 'Little early to be doing the rounds, isn't it?'

The caretaker grinned from the doorway, looking bemusedly from Andrea to Rachel – who was working on a half-organised wall display in the far corner of the hall – before shaking his head. 'It's gone nine, you two. Museum shut hours ago. What are you still doing here?'

'Christ, really?' Andrea said, running a hand through her hair. 'Well, I guess you're off home then, are you?'

'I am,' Darren nodded. 'You all right locking the staff doors after you've gone? I think the boss is still in her office, but she'll likely be off soon.'

Andrea fumbled for the keys in her pocket, jangled them for the caretaker to hear. 'No worries. Thanks, Darren.'

The caretaker threw her a mock salute and backed out of the door, letting it swing shut behind him. Andrea listened for a moment as he wheeled his trolley away down the corridor; only now did she realise that the sounds of the crowds outside the exhibition hall had died down entirely.

Quickly, she turned her head in Rachel's direction. 'You'd better go,' she called, 'I'm so sorry, I didn't realise how late it was. I'll make sure you get overtime for this. For now, you head home and I'll finish up in here.'

Rachel shook her head, gently aligning a bulky black picture frame on the wall. Behind the glass, a rag of papyrus was spattered with odd, blood-red symbols arranged around a five-point star and, in the centre, an ornately-decorated cartouche. 'That's fine,' the girl said, 'I'll stay. You'll be here all night otherwise. At least with an extra pair of hands we might both get home by midnight.'

Andrea moved slowly across the hall, her hands tucked into her pockets. 'Are you sure? I'm not going to ask you to stay, Rach. You've done plenty enough. Time to…'

Rachel turned away from the wall as the older woman trailed off, frowning a little. 'What's—'

Andrea was looking out of the window.

'Are they still there?' Rachel said quietly.

Andrea nodded. She had almost forgotten about them, though the niggling sense of unease had not left her for most of the day. 'They're still there.'

Rachel joined her at the window and they both looked out onto the square below. 'Jesus,' the girl said, 'what the hell are they doing?'

The crowds had dispersed, disappeared, and a thick bank of inky darkness hung across the square, only interrupted by foggy halos of orange lamplight. In that dim light Andrea saw them clearly: the men in orange, monkish robes stood completely moveless, exactly where they had been all day. Hoods pulled over their faces, they stood a few feet from each other in a perfect circle around the building, the closest of them only thirty or thirty-five feet from the front doors.

'I don't know,' Andrea said, 'but I really think you should go—'

Movement suddenly. There was the muffled thud of a door closing and a dull smudge of grey appeared beneath them, barely discernible through the window.

'Is that Darren?'

'Oh, my god,' Andrea whispered. 'What's he doing? Why hasn't he gone out the back?'

Then she had the sudden thought that, if the robed figures were really surrounding the building, they might have blocked the staff doors. Back there, Darren would have seen them through the glass; perhaps he had decided to try the main doors and lock them behind him, not realising that the creepy figures were out the front too.

Beneath them the caretaker stepped out into the square, moving slowly. His hands were stuffed in the pockets of his overalls, and he moved warily, clearly having clocked the monks. For a moment he paused, and then he moved decisively forward with a friendly nod in the nearest monk's direction.

Suddenly the circle closed in.

Andrea gasped as every one of the monks took two steps forward, closing the gaps between them and advancing on the museum. The ring tightened, the hooded figures forming a strangling chokehold on the building's throat.

Darren froze, raising both his hands.

For a moment he just stood there. 'Get inside,' Andrea whispered, 'come on, get inside…'

He took a single step back toward the museum.

The monks closed in again, the gaps between each hooded figure disappearing completely.

Rachel was dialling beside her. Andrea glanced down at the young woman's phone and saw that she had called 999. Hurriedly Rachel raised the phone to her ear. 'Come on…'

Outside, the muffled sound of dialogue. Darren was trying to reason with them. He just wanted to get home. What did they want with him?

'Come on…' Rachel hissed. Then she yelped. Andrea wheeled around, both eyebrows raised in surprise, but already she could hear the loud, piercing shriek coming through the phone and knew that there was no hope of reaching the police.

'Shit,' Andrea said, turning her face back to the window. 'What do we—'

The monks closed in again. She gasped as she caught a flash of silver, clamping a hand over her mouth as the knife was plunged into Darren's gut. Even so far below them she could hear the caretaker grunt as the blade twisted in his stomach, reaching desperately to grab the arm of the monk who had stabbed him and wrench it away.

The knife slid easily out of his body and he wheezed, crumpling to his knees as a jet of ichor streamed from his belly. Beside him, another of the hooded monks grabbed him by the collar of his overalls, holding the swaying man up on his knees. Meanwhile a third reached into the caretaker's pocket and swiped the keys.

They dropped Darren's body effortlessly and he fell, limp, clutching at his stomach to stem the flow of blood. It was useless; it ran into the concrete around him and pooled about his waist as he lay convulsing at their feet.

The first monk slid the knife back into a dark leather belt and threw a casual hand signal toward the others.

'Oh, Jesus,' Rachel breathed as the bulk of them suddenly stormed the front doors, a flood of orange robes and shadowy faces. A couple of them stayed to take care of the body; as Andrea watched, they began to drag Darren away, still twitching.

From directly beneath them, there came the soft *clunk* of the main entrance being unlocked.

'Hide,' Andrea hissed, pulling Rachel back from the window. The poor young woman's face was flush with shock and her mouth was open, but no words came. Her eyes locked on the window, she breathed shallow breaths and watched the window as Darren's body was bundled roughly across the square.

'They… killed him…'

Andrea grabbed her shoulders and shook her lightly. 'Rachel. Enough. Look at me.'

The girl looked, her eyes wide with fright. She was trembling.

'*Hide,*' Andrea said, squeezing her shoulders tight.

'Hide now, and don't come out for anything. Okay?'

Rachel nodded.

'Good girl,' Andrea nodded, giving her a gentle nudge away from the window. Rachel took a couple slow steps back and looked around the room, scanning the half-assembled displays for something to crawl behind. Beneath them, something shattered loudly and a dozen pairs of heels rang on the stone floor, footsteps muffled through layers of concrete. Something else broke, the sound enough to make Andrea cringe.

She glanced back, watched as Rachel disappeared behind a glass cabinet against the wall. For a moment the girl was still visible, her shape distorted and warped through the glass, then her back slid down the wall and she vanished behind the opaque wooden base of the cabinet.

Andrea turned to the doors.

Drawing in a deep breath, she moved quietly across the exhibition hall. Terror pumped something hard and hot and thick through her veins and she supposed it was the same thing that compelled mothers to lift cars off of babies, or whatever it was they were supposed to be able to do. It didn't matter; for now, it was heady and strong enough to keep her on her feet, though she was acutely aware that when it wore off she would crumple into an exhausted heap.

Downstairs, something else shattered. They were ransacking the entrance hall, probably turning over the reception desk in their search for… whatever. Were they thieves? Were they here to burgle the museum? It was the only thing that made sense – but to stand around so conspicuously for most of the day, and to dress in those monk-like robes… she couldn't help but feel that there was more to this than robbery.

She stopped at the door and withdrew the keys from her pocket, slipping one into the lock.

All she had to do was to keep herself and the girl safe for a little while. The museum had insurance. Curran would have a fit – and rightly so – and it was more than possible that Andrea would suffer the brunt of her mother's disappointment. But Andrea had seen those monks kill a man that she knew. And she couldn't worry about protecting any of the exhibits, not when they might kill her or Rachel too.

She paused, key in the lock, letting her head fall against the door. She heard muffled conversation downstairs.

'…spread out,' came a low, muted voice, 'it must be here somewhere. Check everywhere.'

''It'?' Andrea whispered. What were they looking for?

She had a thought suddenly, a dreadful thought: what if the thing they were looking for was in her office?

'Doesn't matter,' she whispered, shutting her eyes, lightly hammering the door with her forehead. She thought of the staff, lying there on her desk, the staff with the bony head and the dazzling green jewel set in its teeth. 'Let them have it. Let them have it. Let them…'

But what if they discovered the same thing about the staff that she had found upon closer inspection? What then? Would they come back?

More voices, at the top of the stairs now. She listened, catching fragments of muffled conversation:

'…probably still packed up…'

'…check the warehouse, it's…'

'…even look like? I don't…'

It was difficult to make anything out, but if she could only hear what they were looking for, if she only knew that it wasn't something in here with her and the girl, then she would know that they were safe.

Just a second, she thought. I'll only listen for a second.

Gently, her hand still on the key in the lock, she twisted the doorknob and opened it a crack, glancing out into the corridor. Much clearer, she heard two voices down the hall:

'…make sure there was nobody left inside?' one of the monks asked.

'Caretaker's usually the last out,' said another flatly. She heard the soft clip of heels on the hard floor, coming closer. Just a moment longer. 'If there's anyone else in here, we'll take care of them. You know what the boss said. No one can know what happened here. Nobody.'

'Brother Shaw took care of the cameras, I presume?'

'On a loop for the next hour. No security in the building. No witnesses.'

'Good. Let's keep it that way.

Andrea's heart stopped. *No witnesses.*

She ducked back into the exhibition hall and closed the door with a soft *click*, turning the key gently in the lock. God, if they came in here, if they found her and Rachel…

'Mum,' she whispered suddenly.

Shit.

Her mother was still in the building. Darren had told her that Curran was still in her office: she had probably been disapprovingly scrutinising some insignificant batch of paperwork when the monks had broken in. She was probably stood with her ear to the office door right now, like Andrea was, listening for any fractured piece of conversation that might tell her just what was going on. But Curran wouldn't settle for hiding and waiting, oh no, she would want to step out into the corridor and confront somebody – she was going to get herself killed.

I have to find her, Andrea thought, make sure she's not doing anything *stupid*—

Without a second thought, Andrea unlocked the

door again and pulled it open.

Two shapes in bright orange robes passed right in front of her.

Andrea ducked back, her breath hitching in her throat. 'Shit,' she gasped, fumbling for the lock, but she was too slow. One of the monks had already seen her and turned from his brother, grinning beneath his hood as he lurched toward the door, and for a fraction of a second all Andrea could see was a shaft of shadow peeling through the open door and the flash of his teeth. She swung the door shut, twisting her whole body out of reach, grabbing the key in the lock – and her fingers clutched uselessly at the air, suddenly throbbing with a pain that she hadn't noticed for the last few minutes but was manifesting right now as a knot of intense heat.

Something heavy slammed itself against the door and it swung open, battering her shoulder and knocking her out of the way. Andrea cried out, turning her body to face the monks as they barged in, already setting her sights on the key in the lock, wheeling forward to slam the door into the nearest man's face and shunt them back out into the corridor—

'Well, what do we have here?' whispered the grinning monk, coming in through the open door and storming toward her. He moved like a wraith, his legs and arms hidden beneath the folds of the fiery orange robes, his body knifing through the air like white-hot wire through cheese. Suddenly his hands were on her, appearing from within his robes and curling around the fabric of her blouse. His teeth smashed together in a face that was otherwise completely bathed in shadow, that awful grin pointed and sharp like the grin of a shark. She couldn't see his eyes but she knew they were flashing too. Knotting his fists into her blouse so tightly that Andrea felt he might bruise her shoulders, the monk leaned close. His breath was warm and meaty. 'What do we have here, indeed?'

Behind him, the second monk slipped into the room, followed by a third. Andrea's heart sunk into her stomach and lay there in a shrivelled, shattered heap. Damn it, she'd been so stupid – why couldn't she have just locked the door and hidden herself away, like she'd asked Rachel to do?

She was more like her mother than she cared to admit. And now she was going to die.

'Over there,' said one of the monks. More came in through the open doors, five, six of them, flooding in like water and spreading around the room. One of them was pointing. Andrea ripped her gaze from the leering face of the grinning monk who'd grabbed her, looked in the direction of the pointing finger—

The sarcophagus.

'No…'

Andrea's stomach turned sickly as monks gathered around the great glass display case in the centre of the room, five of them moving to stand in a small circle around it, their hooded heads bowed down as they glared at the enormous stone coffin within.

The grinning monk turned to one of his brothers. 'Think she'll be any use to us?' he spat.

The second shook his head, glancing up from the sarcophagus. 'No witnesses,' he said, his voice heavy with a Scottish accent and thick with a cold, emotionless lilt. 'Get rid of her.'

'Fine,' the grinning monk said, turning his awful face back to her and tightening his grip. 'Nice meeting you, love.'

'No!' Rachel screamed from across the room, shooting up suddenly from her hiding place behind the cabinet. 'Leave her alone! Leave her—'

Two hooded figures seized the young woman instantly, each curling a hand around one of her arms and slamming her against the wall. There was an awful *crack* as her skull hit the concrete and for a moment Andrea was terrified that Rachel's head might have split open. Her body went limp in the monks' grip and her head lolled forward. 'What have you done?' Andrea yelled, struggling against the grinning monk, scrambling desperately to get past him. 'Put her down!'

Rachel's head shot up suddenly, as though she'd woken from a deep sleep, and immediately her body stiffened and she began to struggle. She was alive. Alive and largely uninjured, Andrea hoped, if a little bruised.

'You leave her out of this,' Andrea hissed, turning back to the grinning monk. He smiled silently down at her. 'She doesn't know anything. She hasn't seen anything. Isn't that right?' she called across the hall.

'Oh, you're tiresome, love, you know that?' said the grinning monk through gritted teeth. His grip tightened again and he lilted back, tipping his head ready to smash his forehead into hers. 'Why don't we *shut* that irritating little mouth of yours—'

'What's going on in here?'

The voice was quiet, soft. The monk's grip loosened immediately at the sound of it and Andrea wriggled free of his fists, staggering away from him as he turned his head toward the open door. In the corner of the exhibition hall, Rachel had stopped struggling; Andrea glanced across and saw that the monks restraining her had softened their hold too.

Andrea looked past the grinning monk's shoulder toward the door and froze.

More of the orange-robed figures had come in so that there must have been at least a dozen in the hall, most of them gathered around the sarcophagus. There were more in the corridor, she saw, their bodies drenched in shadow but clearly turned away from the doors. Were they keeping guard?

In the open doorway, a tall man in long, bright robes stood with his hands clasped before him. His cloak was different to the others, a pale mustard yellow that stood out sorely from the flood of orange around him. His hood had been removed and hung in a thick clump around his shoulders. He was completely bald and clean shaven, his face thin, cheeks sallow and withdrawn. His eyes were an icy, pale blue, sunk into deep pits in his skull but shining and full of youth. He spoke again:

'Have you found the staff?' said the man in yellow robes, addressing nobody in particular.

Andrea glanced in Rachel's direction at the mention of the staff. The young girl swallowed. Softly, Andrea shook her head. Don't, she said with her eyes.

There was silence around them. After a moment, the man in the doorway repeated himself: 'Have you found the staff?'

He stood perfectly still, his hands held delicately before his waist, his head cocked a little to one side. His voice was like honey and he was so softly-spoken that Andrea felt he should not have commanded this much attention from the monks around him; and yet they seemed in awe of him, each one gazing in his direction as though admiring royalty.

The grinning monk stepped forward, bowing his head slightly. 'Not yet, Brother Arkham,' he said, and Andrea noticed that his hands – the same hands which had left the soft flesh between her chest and shoulders bruised and tender – were folded neatly before him as if in prayer. 'But others are searching.'

'What should we do with these two?' said one of the monks holding Rachel, gripping her arm tight again. She winced.

The man in the yellow robes smiled, his eyes fixed on Andrea's. They ripped violently into her, staring right through her skin and into her soul. 'Well, has anybody thought to ask them if they know where the staff is?'

Silence.

'They do work here, after all,' Brother Arkham said, stepping further into the room. Somewhere in the building, something else shattered; Andrea couldn't help but cringe at the sound of glass sprinkling the floor. 'Brother Fletcher, why don't you ask this woman if she knows anything that might be of use to us?'

Brother Fletcher – the monk with the awful grin – turned to her again and opened his mouth.

'We don't,' Andrea said quietly, speaking directly to the man in yellow robes. 'We don't know anything about any staff. We just want to go home.'

Brother Arkham cocked an eyebrow. 'Well, I'm rather afraid I can't allow that,' he said softly. He looked toward the ring of monks around the sarcophagus. They had been standing silently for minutes, completely moveless, like robed statues. Awaiting orders, Andrea realised now; the man in yellow was clearly in charge. 'Brother Hutson. Sister

Giles. Sister Castor. Join the search.'

He turned back to Andrea and smiled.

'After all, we can't open his cage until we've found it, can we?'

Three of the hooded figures slipped out of the hall behind him and disappeared into the corridor. Andrea found that her breath was slowing. They hadn't killed her or Rachel, not yet. There was still a chance. If she could only negotiate with this man, with their leader...

'Now,' Brother Arkham said, stepping closer. 'Brother Fletcher, ask her again if she knows the whereabouts of the staff.'

Across the room, Rachel wriggled in the grip of the two monks at her sides. Andrea caught the young woman's eye, saw that her face had twisted into a desperate and terrified mask. 'I don't know what you're looking for,' Andrea said calmly. 'And I don't know where it is.'

The man in yellow sighed. 'Brother Fletcher, ask her again.'

Brother Fletcher turned to her, grinning once more beneath his hood. 'Gladly,' he whispered.

Before Andrea could react, he bunched his knuckles into a thick, tight fist and punched it into her throat. She stumbled back a step, reaching up to clutch at her neck, gasping for air as it was sucked out of her chest. She drew in frantic breaths, crumpling to her knees, a thick patch of heat spreading across her throat and

107

chin.

'I… can't…' she gasped. 'Can't… breathe…'

Brother Arkham simply looked down at her from across the room, his face still, and Andrea noticed that his nose was crooked and bent, making him look a little like a vulture. Brother Fletcher towered over her, his fist cocked like a weapon.

Andrea shook her head, staggering to her feet and swaying, one hand clamped over her throat and massaging it. 'Don't… know… anything…'

'Leave her alone!' Rachel screamed, bolting forward suddenly. The monks grabbing her moved swiftly, two streaks of orange yanking her back and slamming her into the wall again.

'Ask her again,' Brother Arkham said quietly, ignoring the younger woman's outburst.

The grinning monk launched his fist into Andrea's stomach, sending a pulse of agony up her spine. She doubled over, gasping raggedly. 'I don't know anything,' she breathed, 'please…'

The man in the yellow robes shook his head. 'Ask her again.'

Fletcher drew back his fist.

'No!' Rachel shrieked. 'We know where the staff is, all right?'

Andrea shook her head, a mess of hair in her eyes. 'No,' she moaned, her voice barely a whisper, 'don't…'

Brother Fletcher lowered his fist.

Slowly, the man in yellow robes turned to Rachel, his lips stretched into a thin, cruel smile. 'Oh, really?' he said. 'And where is it?'

'Don't,' Andrea whispered. 'Rachel, don't tell them—'

'Shut her up,' Arkham snapped.

Brother Fletcher leaned down and grabbed her by the blouse, hauling her to her feet, and before she could untangle herself from him he had clamped a hand over her mouth, the flesh of his palm sweaty and hot. She shook her head frantically but her neck was caught in the crook of his arm and he was too strong.

'Tell us,' Brother Arkham said quietly. 'Where is it?'

Rachel looked from Andrea to the yellow-robed man and back again. 'I'm sorry,' she whispered.

'Don't,' Andrea cried, but her voice was muffled by the meat of Brother Fletcher's hand. She struggled uselessly.

'It's in her office,' Rachel whispered.

'Is that so?' Brother Arkham said softly, turning his head back toward Andrea. 'Well, thank you both for your cooperation. Brother Lester?'

One of the orange-robed monks stepped forward, bowing his head slightly.

'Go and find the office,' Brother Arkham said. 'Bring me the staff.'

He smiled, and the thin crack that split across his face was a million times worse than Brother Fletcher's gurning, smashed-teeth grin.

'Tonight,' Brother Arkham said softly. 'It all happens tonight.'

Chapter 9

Dr Irene Curran had not planned to be at the museum beyond five o'clock that evening, nor on microwaving a chicken-flavoured NoodleBowl at eight-thirty and bringing it back to her office to see her through the next few hours. Now, of course, she couldn't imagine leaving the building before eleven.

But it was all true: the English Historical Museum had a deep, red wound in its gut and blood and money spilled from it at a rate that she knew she couldn't control, no matter how many late nights she spent fussing over budgets and schedules and loan proposals. She had rather understated the issue when she'd seen Andrea and Dr Phillips in her office: the museum wasn't just bleeding out slowly, it was dying quite violently in her arms, and there was nothing that any of them could do about it.

She sat at her desk and stared at paperwork until the words on the page became little more than a haze of smudged shapes, and then she leant back in her chair and stared at the ceiling. The dishwater smell of the empty noodle container wafted into her nostrils and made her vaguely queasy. She'd had other plans for tonight – and what had been the point in postponing them? She hadn't achieved anything by staying, hadn't changed anything…

Absent-mindedly she scrambled in the top drawer of her desk and pulled out two tabs of pills. She swallowed two painkillers for the headache and popped a single dapoxetine for the rest of it. She had plucked out the in-ear headphones that had been drilling Bach into her skull for the last hour and they hung around her neck, pumping out a tinny abomination of sound that she could just barely hear above the frantic ticking of the antique clock on the wall.

Leaning forward to tilt open her laptop, Curran entered the password and opened her e-mails. There was a new message from Andrea's father, and she read it quickly:

No need to apologise, these things happen. We'll talk another night.

She sat back again, folding her knuckles against her chin and musing over the e-mail. Well, perhaps they would, but she had a feeling that every setback she allowed to creep between them further stalled the progress they'd been making over the last few months. How was she supposed to save a marriage that had been undone for years *and* a museum that was dramatically bleeding out around her?

There was no way, and every day that passed she came closer to the realisation that she might have to choose.

Andrea would know what to say, she thought bitterly.

She shook her head of the thought and popped the headphones back into her ears, the low, rumbling oboe blasts of Bach's *Magnificat* thrumming into the bones of her skull. She puffed air through her cheeks and drew the mobile phone from her pocket. That was quite enough of that; she found her favourite Stones album and pressed play.

In the brief, silent fragment of a moment between songs, there was a sound from somewhere in the museum like the slamming of a door. She frowned, her finger hovering over the phone screen as *Gimme Shelter* filled her ears. Probably nothing. She glanced at the time; must have been Darren leaving the building.

Curran wondered if Andrea was still here. She could make her way to the exhibition hall where her daughter was working, pull her aside to talk about everything. About her attempts at repairing the rift between herself and the girl's father; about the museum; about maybe starting to fix the damage between the two of them and trying to be a family again.

No. Where was the use in talking about all that? She thought about it all enough, and it only ever brought her to tears.

She returned to the loan proposal, her ears filled with music, and tilted her head forward to squint over the writing. She had printed the document to read it through one more time, and the top half of the page was covered in red handwritten amendments; in the morning, she'd fix the document on her laptop and send it away.

This one had to be accepted. Surely.

She jolted as a loud *thump* echoed somewhere in the building. Looking up and toward the closed door of her office, Curran removed one of the headphones and listened intently.

Nothing.

Just Andrea scrambling over the last few items on her tick-list, she thought. And perhaps she'd be more use out there, helping her daughter put the exhibit together ready for tomorrow, than she was in here fussing over everything she couldn't fix.

'God, what a mess,' she moaned quietly, running a hand through her hair as she returned her attention to the desk. 'What a fucking disaster, Irene.'

She popped the headphone back in and reached for her laptop, swiping at the trackpad to wake it up again. She refreshed her e-mails, almost hoping that he had sent her another message. *Forget about work for one night,* it would say, *I'm coming to whisk you away. Let's go to France, like we did for our honeymoon. You remember? Let's go to France and eat all the shit we can't pronounce and forget about everything else, and let's take her with us this time so she can see what all the fuss was about.*

There was nothing new in her inbox.

She refreshed the screen again.

Footsteps, right outside the door. Ringing on the stone flags loud enough for her to hear through the chorus of *Country Honk.* Curran wheeled toward the door and stumbled out of her chair, dragging both headphones out of her ears and letting them hang around her throat.

Moving quickly to the door, she pressed her ear to the wood and listened for any sign of movement in the corridor. For a full minute she stood, most of that time holding her breath, and waited.

Absolutely nothing. She was going mad.

She returned the headphones to her ears and stepped back across to the desk. Flopping down into her seat, she laid her head in her hands and drew in a deep breath. She needed to sleep. This could all wait. She could go home, get into bed. Forget about it.

Forget about it.

'Ugh,' she said loudly, tipping her head up and sniffling to clear the build-up in her nose. She could feel the tears coming on but wouldn't let them, not tonight. 'Get a grip, woman. Get on with it.'

Something in the corner of her eye. Something wrong.

Her body frozen in the chair, Dr Irene Curran let out a shallow breath and slowly dragged her eyes to one side. Looked sidelong at the door.

It was wide open. The corridor outside was dark. The door was completely still on its hinges; there was nobody out there. It had been open for a few moments, at least.

Quietly, carefully, Curran reached for the headphones and plucked them finally from her ears. Every movement was slow and calculated; next she reached, inch-by-inch, for the phone and, without looking at it, dialled the volume down to zero to silence the tinny rattling around her neck.

She could almost feel the bones in her neck creaking as she turned her head and looked around the office. She sniffed; the sickly scent of the NoodleBowl was gone, replaced by the tang of washed pennies.

Her office was empty.

She breathed a sigh of relief, turning a full circle in her office chair to make sure she hadn't missed some balaclava-wearing thief standing in the corner of the room. There was nobody here but her. Slowly, she stood up to close the door. Must have swung open on its own. Old lock had finally busted open. That was all.

Something *plopped* onto her desk.

She looked down and frowned at the red-penned document. A splodge of crimson ink had splashed the corner of the page, tiny dots of it spattered around the mark. Funny. She didn't remember the pen leaking. Another smell had lilted into the room and she cringed: it smelled like decay, like meat rotting.

As she stared at the paper, another drop landed upon it.

Plop.

Curran's eyes widened and she looked up.

And she screamed as the grey-skinned creature leapt, springing from its place on the ceiling and yawing its smashed teeth wide open as it pounced upon her.

Brother Fletcher stood behind Andrea and pinned her arms behind her back, breathing hot air into her neck. He was pressed closely enough to her that she could almost feel his heartbeat through his robes, hear saliva churning in his mouth.

Beside her, another of the monks held Rachel in a similar position. The younger woman struggled violently but the monk – a thin, tan man with a neatly-trimmed beard and sharp green eyes that Andrea had only glimpsed very briefly beneath his hood – was stronger than his slender frame would have suggested. He grunted quietly as he restrained her, twisting her wrists carelessly. Andrea glanced sidelong at the girl and shook her head. The monks hadn't injured either of them too badly, not yet. There was no sense in making them any angrier than they were.

Brother Arkham was pacing before the sarcophagus when Brother Lester and a lithe, female monk returned to the exhibition hall with the staff from Andrea's office. She winced as she saw it, the green jewel at its crest glittering. She wondered if they already knew what she'd discovered about the thing. Surely not, she thought.

Surely not, or they wouldn't be here.

'Excellent,' Arkham said, knotting his bony hands together. He smiled thinly in Andrea's direction before turning his attention to the staff. 'What a... marvellously *opulent* thing.'

Rachel had stopped struggling. 'What are you doing?' she hissed, a mess of black hair in her face. 'Why won't you let us go?'

Arkham raised a thin hand to silence her. He wheeled back toward the sarcophagus, pivoting on his heels so that his yellow robes whorled behind him. The fluorescent lights above peppered his bald head with spangles of white and he stood there for a moment, commanding the attention of every hooded figure in the room without saying a word. There must have been a couple dozen of them, Andrea noted, each one absolutely fixated on the man. A ring of them surrounded the sarcophagus, still lying silently in its own glass case; more stood around the edges of the room, heads bowed, waiting.

Brother Arkham clenched his fist suddenly and the hall exploded into chaos.

Immediately one of the monks beside the sarcophagus extended a hand, withdrawing a thick metal spike from his robes. He punched the butt of the thing into the glass case, right in the middle of the pane, and it shattered loudly. A shower of glass shards caved in and sprinkled the sarcophagus and Andrea yelped, her stomach turning in her throat. She wriggled but Brother Fletcher tightened his grip, his breath so loud in her ear that she fancied she could hear him growling like a dog. Two more of the monks followed the example of the first and produced metal spikes of their own, swinging the flat ends into the side panels of the glass casing until every pane was smashed. At the other end of the room, the door swung shut and slammed loudly. The monks had begun to chant, and their voices lilted over the kaleidoscopic ruin of sound as Andrea watched, wide-eyed:

'*Venit vivificantem. Excitamus te. Laudamus te!*'

'What are they saying?' Rachel yelled as the chanting rose in volume and cycled around, around, around.

'I don't know!' Andrea called back, struggling against Fletcher's grip. 'Phillips would know—'

She managed to wrench her arm free and thrust it forward, but he was fast, grabbing her elbow and snapping it back. 'Hold still, cow,' he hissed in her ear.

'Fuck off,' she snapped back.

'*Venit vivificantem! Excitamus te! Laudamus te!*'

Four of the monks moved silently to the lid of the sarcophagus, standing shoulder-to-shoulder. Each one held an iron spike in one hand and raised their eyes to the ceiling.

'*VENIT VIVIFICANTEM! EXCITAMUS TE! LAUDAMUS TE!*'

'Enough!' Brother Arkham called above the noise, and the chanting ceased.

The silence was incredible.

'What the hell do you want?' Andrea whispered breathlessly. He turned to look in her direction and his eyes were on fire. 'Whatever's in that box,' she continued, 'it's dead. Long dead.'

'Oh, not quite,' Arkham said calmly.

Rachel shook her head. 'Are you fucking stupid? It's thousands of years old, and he was dead when they put him in there!'

'Perhaps,' Arkham said. He paused for a moment, then turned to the younger woman. 'What do you know of the man in the sarcophagus?'

Rachel glanced desperately at Andrea, who shook her head quietly. *Don't.*

'Tell me,' Arkham said, stepping closer to the girl.

Her dark eyes flashed angrily. The monk smiled. 'Tell me what you think is in there.'

'There were pictures,' Rachel said quietly, carefully. 'In the book. The magician. But they killed him – with the staff'—she looked in the direction of the thing, then turned back to him—'they made him kill himself. But even if they'd buried him alive, he'd be long dead by now. What could you want with a corpse?'

'Hmm,' Arkham murmured. Leaning forward, he said, 'Did she tell you what kind of sorcerer he was?'

Rachel shook her head.

Arkham shrugged, looking slyly in Andrea's direction. 'I don't suppose it would have mattered. Perhaps she hadn't managed to translate anything that would have told her just what kind of magic the dead man had been involved with.'

Andrea swallowed. There was something about the way he said the word 'dead' – something coy and knowing, like a lie – that she hated. That she feared. The sarcophagus was still, silent, but the shadows creeping around the edge of the lid seemed to have grown deeper.

'Or perhaps she didn't think it worth telling,' Arkham said, finally turning back to the sarcophagus. 'After all, there's no such thing as *magic*.'

'Let us go,' Andrea whispered.

'But our friend in the box isn't dead,' the monk said,

ignoring her. 'He never was. Not really.'

Andrea looked bewildered at the man, then at the staff. 'Then what good d'you think you'll do with that thing?'

'Oh, we're not here to kill him,' Arkham said. 'We're here to control him.'

He raised his hand again. As one, the four monks standing beside the sarcophagus slammed the tapered ends of their metal spikes into the opening and pressed forward with their hands, putting their whole weight into the movement.

There was an awful sound of stone grinding stone and the lid budged less than an inch. For a moment Andrea was relieved, then all four of them withdrew the spikes and slammed them forward again, each of them grunting loudly. The lid scraped itself another couple of inches.

Again they plunged the stubby iron spears into the opening and pushed forward, and again the lid slid back. Andrea saw the monk with the staff straightening a little, bracing himself. Arkham did not react; his face was a mask of patience.

A fourth strike, and a fifth, and sixth, each one accompanied by that awful scream of granite on granite, and then a narrow slit had opened at the edge of the sarcophagus. Barely a dozen inches wide, but enough. Wordlessly slipping the spikes back into their robes, all four monks thrust their hands into the narrow black cavern and gripped the underside of the lid. There was a beat, then they rocked their arms upward. The lid barely wobbled, and the weight of it drew their forearms down again. Up they rocked a second time, and this time it threatened to tip.

As they rocked the lid a third time, it slid off the sarcophagus with a shriek of stone and crashed to the floor, scattering glass fragments.

The great stone tomb was open.

Chapter 10

'Be prepared!' Brother Arkham yelled. There was a ruffle of fabric as each of the monks filed around the edges of the room unsheathed a long, flat knife from their robes. The one holding the staff, Brother Lester, swung it forward and pointed the bony head of the thing toward the open sarcophagus. Andrea drew in a hard breath and held it.

Nothing happened.

Half a minute passed before Brother Arkham took a single step forward, drawing a knife from his own robes. 'Come on,' she heard him whisper, 'show yourself...'

She had half-expected a bony hand to thrust out of the dark and grip the edge of the coffin, or for some grinning, skeletal figure to lurch up and snap its teeth at her. But there was nothing. No movement; just the dark sucking light off the particles of dust that floated above it, and the smell of blood.

Andrea laughed softly. 'Christ,' she said. 'You

really had me going there. I practically thought something was going to climb out of that thing and swipe at us.'

'Something's wrong,' Rachel whispered.

Andrea shook her head. 'Yeah, you don't say,' she said quietly, hardly noticing that Brother Fletcher's grip on her arms had loosened and that he was holding his whole body stiff with anticipation. 'This is insane.'

'No, I mean... can't you smell it?' Rachel hissed.

Andrea paused. Nothing except the smell of sweat in the room and the thick stench of death coming from the sarcophagus.

The thick, *fresh* stench of death.

'Shit,' Andrea whispered, just as Brother Arkham reached the sarcophagus and looked down into it.

'Search the museum!' he yelled suddenly, whirling around, his eyes darting from corner to corner. 'Now!'

Fletcher let go of Andrea's arms and backed away. She took her chance and lurched forward, hurtling awkwardly toward the sarcophagus. The monks who had opened it had scattered around the hall now and a knot of orange robes flooded toward the doors. 'What is it?' she yelled. 'What's in—'

She looked down into the dark and balked.

Jez lay mangled in the sarcophagus, his arms and legs twisted and snapped at such horrendous angles that for a fleeting moment Andrea thought some animal's carcass had been smashed into the stone. But his face was clean, almost completely untouched, and his wide eyes were fixed on her, his mouth open in a silent and horrified scream, and she almost felt that his skull had been left intact just to mess with her, because the rest of him…

'Oh, Jez, I'm so sorry,' she whispered, covering her mouth. The sickly sweet smell of decay bloomed off his body and filled her throat. His neck was snapped and rent open, his guts savaged, pooling out of a ruptured stomach. His clothes were in tatters, his body scorn through with thick, swollen gashes. Blood pooled out of him and into the basin of the sarcophagus, flooding around his awkwardly-bent knees and ankles.

She should have known something was wrong when Karl had told her the boy hadn't come into work, she should have *known*…

But how could she? God, who the hell could have done this to him?

Out in the corridor, somebody screamed. There was a sound like a wellington boot sucked into a thick patch of muck, and then a soft *thwump*. Andrea looked toward the doors; one of the monks had reached the handle, and wrenched it open; her eyes snapped wide open as a blood-smeared blur streaked past the doorway and disappeared into the dark.

Across the room, Rachel shrieked. She had a better view of the corridor, Andrea realised, staggering forward. There was something out there.

Her eyes dropped to the floor.

There had been two monks guarding the door, and now there were two orange-robed bodies laying just outside of it, both completely still.

Brother Arkham grabbed Andrea by the arm and yanked her back. 'Don't fucking move,' he rasped, spittle flying from his lips.

Andrea barely noticed him. 'Shut the doors!' she yelled as the monk who'd opened them poked his head out into the corridor. 'Shut the fucking doors!'

The monk turned back, shaking his head. 'I don't see anything, boss,' he called to Brother Arkham. 'It must have—'

A tiny yelp escaped his mouth as something grabbed the monk by the throat and snatched him out into the hall. There was a sick, dry *crack* and something else: the sound of something feasting, of pig snouts slopping in a bucket of scraps, and Andrea knew that the thing that had whipped him so easily forward into the dark was eating him.

'Shut the doors,' she said again, her voice terrible and quiet.

'Defend yourselves!' Brother Arkham yelled, his presence suddenly the imposing forcefulness of a military man, and Andrea wondered for the first time how he'd gotten here, what the hell he was doing – what *any* of them were doing – breaking into museums at night looking for dead wizards.

All around them, the robed figures braced themselves, taking wide, defensive stances, lowering their hoods to better see their attacker. For the first time Andrea noticed that there was a metallic rattling sound whenever they moved, and saw that their robes bulged about the ribs and waist, as though the body beneath were laden; they were carrying far more than knives, she realised. As she watched, one of them removed a thick steel pole from her robes and extended the telescopic end of it; a thick loop of steel cable swung back as she braced the pole and Andrea was reminded of the kind of noose that she'd seen used to capture an alligator or crocodile on television.

Andrea ripped her eyes from the door and shook her head. 'Why are you doing this?' she said. Out in the corridor, the thing had finished chewing, and the sounds of meat popping in its jaws had stopped. There was a bitter silence, followed by a soft, padding footstep, a slap of bone into blood. It was coming. 'Why did you come here? How did you even *know* to come here? The staff, the sarcophagus – how did you know they were here?'

'Don't you know?' Arkham said, smiling grimly back at her. 'Your *friend* told us.'

Chapter 11

'Hello?' Bruce called quietly as he came around the back of the museum building. The square had been completely empty, and though usually there were some signs of life in the flickering lights that shot through the windows behind the building, tonight there seemed none at all. Often there might be one or two smokers gathered around the glass door that served as a staff entrance. Tonight, nobody. The dark air was eerie and cloying. 'Hello? Anyone?'

Realising he was alone out here, he unfolded himself from the dark. He was dressed in one of his sharper suits, an oceanic blue blazer to match his pleated trousers, a glaring orange waistcoat that flashed bloody in the pale, flickering light coming from within the corridor beyond the door. Body straightening a little, Bruce steeled himself and stepped up to the door, raising his thumb to jab the buzzer.

He paused.

He hadn't been able to tell at first, what with the clear glass and the dark spattering of shadow behind it, but the door was wide open.

Bruce swallowed. Glanced behind him to see if there was anybody about. Nothing; he couldn't even hear the usual thrum of activity from the direction of the warehouse, though the yellow hue of the floodlights seeped over a low brick wall to his left.

'Well, then,' Bruce said, 'in we go.'

He stepped inside through the open door and closed it gently behind him.

There was a bolt of grey as the creature crashed into the hall, barrelling into two of the hooded figures nearest the door. Rachel screamed, ripping herself out of the grip of the tan monk who'd been holding her. The girl scrambled toward the sarcophagus and Andrea grabbed her by the arms to steady her. Rachel's body tipped a little and she screamed again as she saw the contents of the sarcophagus. Briskly, Andrea turned her away from it and pulled her close, never taking her eyes off the thing in the doorway.

'We have to go,' she said, as calmly as possible. Her heart was pounding in her chest, blood thumping in her ears. She took Rachel's hand in her own and shook her head. 'We have to get out of here.'

In the doorway, the creature bent up its head and screeched up at the ceiling. Then it grinned madly at the monks surrounding it, each brandishing a flat-bladed knife or one of the metal stakes which had been used to open the thing's sarcophagus. The gurning maw of the thing was a mess of mashed bone punched into a withered, flaking jaw. Blood streamed from its mouth in thick, gluey strings. Crouched over the nearest limp body it turned its head, scanning every one of the monks' faces intently, and a dull, stony rattle echoed from within its sallow throat.

The grin never left its face as it looked around, a gritted wall of tooth and bone stretched into a colourless smile and plastered into its skull. The monks surrounding it were still, completely moveless, as though trapped in their places by its eerie gaze.

For a moment it caught Andrea's eye and she saw that the dim lights in the sockets of its skull were a burning green.

The creature's whole body shifted as it sloughed off the bewildered stares of everyone in the room and dipped its head back into the feast at its feet. It moved like a starved animal, punching its jaws into the throat of the dead monk and ripping flesh away in chunks, tossing them back into its mouth and swallowing without chewing. It might have been a man once, but now it was a monster; its body was malnourished and grey, the bones clearly visible through skin that was impossibly thin. Its flesh was bruised and glossy in places as if smeared with tar, or with some metallic paste, and Andrea wondered if all that shine was blood. Its arms and legs were slender, yet looked powerful, the skin tightly pressed to angular bones with scraps of striated muscle patching the pieces together. The thing's back was hunched and its spine was a series of mottled bumps, like the spines of some carnivorous dinosaur; its shoulders and joints were impossibly sharp and as it slopped its jaw in the bloody mess of the monk's throat, its entire body quivered and writhed. Long, grotty fingers dug into the sunken pit of the poor man's stomach and ripped out chunks of intestine, working like claws.

Its head was little more than a thin mask of skin stretched tight across a bulging, cracked skull. The green points of its eyes rolled madly in pitch-black sockets; its nose was caved in and hollow; its cheeks were non-existent, the bony lengths of its jaw drawing straight up into the corners of bone beneath its eyes. The creature was decorated with scraps of cloth and jewellery: where once a thick, red cloak had streamed from its shoulders, now a meagre bundle of crimson fabric, stiff with the dried, encrusted fluid that had preserved it for so many centuries, hung from its throat like a ragged scarf. Another scrap of red cloth coiled around its waist, only half-covering the mutilated agony of its groin.

Its wrists were decorated with sharp, gold bangles, dulled by time so that they looked like stone, each one inlaid with an intricate web of engravings. A thick, circular pendant was pinned to its chest, also carved ornately with patterns and characters in a language that Andrea couldn't hope to understand, but one that she recognised from the pages of the book.

This was him. The magician, somehow revived in this awful, animalistic form.

And he was an abomination.

'Now!' Brother Arkham yelled.

The creature looked up from its bloody meal as the crowd of monks around it parted, splitting in two like the red sea. Brother Lester charged forward, the staff with the bony head and the fused, green jewel held forward like a fishing harpoon. 'The power is ours now, you insolent thing!' Lester yelled, his voice booming across the room. 'You will obey m—'

The bony thing leapt up and pounced like a wildcat, punching the entire weight of its body into Brother Lester and smashing him into the ground. Andrea clamped a hand over her mouth as the staff skittered from the man's arms and slid across the floor; the creature was a blur of movement, pounding its clawed hands into the monk's face and throat and chest, screeching like a baboon as it drew massive ribbons of blood from the poor man's flesh, ripping and rending and punching great welts into Lester's skull. The monk's body twitched, fingers curling and uncurling uselessly, as the creature smashed its knuckles – rows upon rows of them knotted together – into his face again and again and again, punching and clawing and savaging until all that was left of Brother Lester's top half was a wet, tender slab of meat. The bones of his chest had caved in and thick gobs of blood pooled out of him in throbbing, red waves.

Somebody else screamed as the creature punched a bone-grey fist into the man's chest and wrenched something loose. As it yanked Lester's spine up out of his ribcage, the monk's entire body convulsed one last time, and then stopped.

There was a clattering sound as somebody bent to pick up the staff. The creature spun around and looked in the direction of the noise.

'Now,' Andrea said, squeezing Rachel's hand. 'Let's go.'

Brother Arkham shook his head. 'You're not going anywhere,' he hissed, wheeling around suddenly and slamming the heel of his hand into her chin. Andrea's teeth slammed together and her head tipped back, stars shooting across her vision as she sprawled backward. Rachel's hand slipped out of hers as her calves hit the stone sarcophagus, and she crumpled onto her knees, swaying for a moment.

Through the blurry haze of her vision she saw an orange-robed woman brandish the staff, her face a tight mask of fury beneath a hood that had largely come undone to reveal a thick knot of red hair.

'It won't work,' Andrea croaked, scrambling to her feet. 'The staff, it won't—'

The woman holding the staff screamed something in a language that sounded like Latin, but wasn't. She braced herself against the weapon as though expecting a rocket to launch from its tip, squeezing her eyes shut.

Nothing happened.

Arkham's eyes flashed with anger and confusion. Andrea watched as the red-haired woman looked desperately in his direction, then turned back to the creature.

It stood over Brother Lester's body, long, thin arms hanging by its sides, skull smeared with blood. Slowly, it cocked its head quizzically to one side. Andrea saw that it had once been embalmed, its body wrapped with gauze, and that tiny flakes of the stuff clung to its back where, she supposed, they had been pressed into the skin through decades and decades of lying against the stone floor of the sarcophagus. Once, the dead thing had been mummified; now all that remained was the withered husk that had decayed within the bandages.

The woman with the staff jabbed it toward the creature, screaming again in that unknown, ancient language, just a single word, steadying her whole body as though she expected the room to start shaking.

But the staff was silent. It did nothing, a useless tool

of metal and bone in her hands.

Another sickly rattle crackled in the mummy's throat, and it lurched forward.

The woman screamed as it batted the staff from her hands, smacking it halfway across the room where it slammed into one of the displays and dropped like a lead weight. Another of the monks lurched forward, withdrawing a long, brass chain from his robes and brandishing it with both hands as though preparing to garotte the creature.

'Leave her alone!' Andrea yelled, but the mummy couldn't hear her – or chose not to – and bore down on the poor woman, thrusting both of its bony thumbs quickly and effortlessly into her eyeballs and lunging in to rip open her throat with its teeth as hot, white jelly streamed down her face. A bright, red jet of blood sprayed the floor and a ten-tonne silence crushed the woman's scream and killed it instantly.

The silence lasted a beat, and then movement rippled through the monks and they closed in on the awful bone-grey thing, knives and stakes flashing. 'The staff, idiots!' yelled Brother Arkham. 'Don't kill it – oh, for fuck's sake, if you need something doing—'

As he lurched for the staff, Andrea shook her head. 'It won't work,' she called after him.

Across the room, the first orange-robed figure, a dark-skinned woman with a shaved head and strange, ancient symbols tattooed across her neck, lashed at the creature with her knife. The blade sunk into its shoulder and a tiny cloud of dust erupted around the handle. The woman moved quickly, twisting the knife hard clockwise and withdrawing it in a single fluid flick of her wrist, but the mummy was quicker; it thrust its claws up into her belly and punched hard into her stomach, spraying blood up the folds of her robes. A second monk was already attacking, and a third, and as the second swiped blindly at the mummy's face with his knife the third swung the blunt end of her stake into the back of its knee, jolting its body forward.

Brother Arkham whirled round, one hand reaching for the bone-headed spear, the other pointing furiously at Andrea. 'What the fuck do you mean, it won't work?' he hissed.

The mummy roared, its throat rattling with a deathly, low rumble infused with millennia of hatred. It slammed a bony elbow back into the second monk's face and the wet *crack* of the man's nose resounded as he took a stumbling step back. Wheeling around, the creature snatched the stake easily from the third attacker's hand and jabbed it forward, hard, moving not like an animal anymore but like a trained soldier, a warrior; the fierce point of the spike was driven into the woman's chest and she gasped as it sunk quickly between her ribs.

'Don't you know?' Andrea croaked, her eyes on the

carnage, her voice so weak that she could not have possibly conveyed the same smugness that Arkham had when he'd asked her the same question, even if she'd wanted to.

'Know what?' Arkham snapped, bending to swipe the staff from the floor. But he faltered even before she responded, pausing as he noticed the same thing that she'd seen in her office:

'It's a fake,' she called. 'It won't work because it's a replica – it's a fucking fake, arsehole!'

Brother Arkham froze. A rain of blades beat down on the mummy's head and back and it screeched, grabbing one monk by the throat and sliding all of its bony fingers easily into the flesh of the man's neck, ripping out a visceral spray of gore and letting the corpse fall limp at its feet.

'It's a fake,' Andrea whispered. In all the chaos, the staff clattered loudly to the floor, and when Brother Arkham looked back up at them his eyes were on fire.

Chapter 12

Arkham bundled them forcefully into the corridor and slammed the door behind them. Immediately the lock clicked and he wheeled around, bearing down on Andrea with fury on his face. 'You knew!' he seethed through gritted teeth. 'You fucking knew, you hag!'

'Oh, god,' Rachel balked, stepping over one of the bodies sprawled across the stone floor of the corridor. There were three orange-robed corpses immediately outside the door, and another two farther down the hall. One lay with its arms broken and twisted above its head, and the other was slumped against the wall, ribbons of red running down from a ragged hole where the left side of its torso had been. 'What the hell is happening?'

Three of the monks had made it out of the exhibition hall with them. Flat-bladed knives flashed in the dark as they slid the weapons back into their robes, ignoring the muffled sounds of the carnage coming from behind the door.

'We need somewhere defensible,' one of the monks said. Andrea glanced in his direction and saw that it was Brother Fletcher; her stomach twisted sickly. 'A room with only one entrance.'

'Never mind that,' Arkham growled, thundering toward Andrea. Inside the exhibition hall, the creature roared, slamming something against the wall. A shrill cry of agony broke up and turned to gargling and Andrea heard something soft and fleshy wrench open. 'You knew the staff was a fake. You understand that renders this entire operation pointless? You understand every single person in that room is going to die now?'

'You brought them here,' Andrea hissed, anger boiling in her veins. 'What, did your *friend* not think to tell you that it wasn't real? Or were they just too dumb to check?'

Arkham swallowed.

'Or were *you* too dumb to ask them?' she spat. 'I don't know what the hell your goal was, Baldy, but you came in here with some dodgy info and some – quite frankly – really *small* knives, and *you* were the ones who knew there was some bone-headed monster in that box, not me! Listen to all the people dying in there right now! That's your fault, you know – and you just *left* them there. You're a fucking monster, you bald piece of—'

'Hold your tongue, woman,' Arkham said. 'My brothers and sisters knew what they signed up for.

Every one of them. They knew the danger.'

'Did they know you'd lock them in there with that monster?'

'Shut up,' Rachel whispered.

Arkham fumed, turning on her. 'You dare,' he hissed, 'you insolent little—'

'No, I mean it. Shut up.' She raised her hand. 'Listen.'

For a moment, Arkham went silent. In the gloom of the bloody corridor, they listened.

The sounds of chaos in the exhibition hall had stopped.

'We have to move,' one of the robed figures said. A broad-shouldered woman with straight, blonde hair falling out of her hood. Her face was grim.

'There's still a chance we can subdue it,' Arkham said. 'Without the staff, there's still a chance.'

Andrea examined his sunken face, unable to tell if he was lying. 'Sure,' she said quietly, glancing at Rachel. The younger woman shook her head; they could try to leave, but that was no safe bet. No safer than staying with the monks. After all, if the mummy came after them, this lot at least had their knives.

'Somewhere defensible,' Brother Fletcher said again. 'Now.'

Andrea nodded reluctantly. 'Hall of Pleistocene Mammals,' she said after a beat. 'Downstairs. Only entrance is from the lobby. Closest room to us with a single door.'

And the closest to the entrance of the building, she thought, our best exit – as long as we make it through the next few minutes.

'Come, then,' Arkham said quietly. 'Lead the way.'

The third monk glanced nervously toward the door of the exhibition hall, the eerie silence beyond it growing more cloying and dangerous with every passing second.

'This way,' Rachel whispered, and the girl led them down the hall, stepping over another mangled carcass on her way.

Andrea's eyes flitted up to the ceiling as something skittered loudly above the tiles. Probably just a rat in the ventilation pipes.

Probably.

The Hall of Pleistocene Mammals was an eerie, labyrinthine hive of soft blue lamplight and monstrous silhouettes. Entering the high-ceilinged room through the archway coming off the museum foyer, they pressed forward into a room split in two: both the long, outwardly-curved walls were crammed with dioramic scenery and great stuffed beasts, and in the centre, like a kitchen island scaled up half a dozen times, a prehistoric landscape was modelled atop a raised circular platform. The ink-black glassy eyes of enormous antediluvian creatures leered down at them, blue flecks of light bouncing off them like sparks of sunlit water off smooth, polished shells.

'This place is so much creepier in the dark,' Rachel whispered as she and Andrea led the monks around one side of the central display.

Andrea said nothing, but internally she screamed at the stupidity of her decision. So many rooms in the museum had only one entrance; why hadn't she taken them to the Gallery of Modern Art? The only creepy thing in there was a sculpture in one corner of a wiry copper-coloured man's torso writhing free of a glossy, white sheet of acrylic spread over the floor that looked like a pool of milk.

Here, they were surrounded by monsters.

As they moved down the right-hand alleyway, keeping the central display on their left, they had to duck around thick tails in mid-swing and great curved tusks that protruded dangerously just above head-height. To their right, on an expansive plateau of faux moss and stone, three sabre-toothed cats stood frozen over the flailing body of an Irish elk. Perfectly still, the carnivores stood with their paws raised, teeth bared, one of them bowed down to rip into the belly of the sprawled beast. A chunk of the scale model's stomach had been ripped out and painted red; the screen behind the diorama was painted with a beautiful sunset, low mountains smeared and scraped with grey. As they headed to the back of the room, a giant ground sloth and a small family of glyptodonts – oddly-shaped, heavily-armoured armadillos – watched them with blank faces and cool, wickedly-glinting eyes.

At the end of the room Andrea turned, standing in the shadow of an enormous, bear-like *Megatheriidae* skeleton – a gargantuan sloth that stood almost three times her height, its fat bony fingers extended, its maw open wide.

Two of the monks – Brother Fletcher and the blonde woman – had slipped around the left side of the central display, and moved among cave lions and short-faced bears toward a small pack of Pleistocene wolves, black lips pulled back from carbon fibre teeth. The creatures were lithe and shadowy in the dark, only their glassy eyes and serrated fangs lit by the pale blue lamps around the edges of the room, and in this half-darkness they looked twice as real as in the day.

'Fascinating stuff,' Brother Arkham said drily, looking up at the colossal beast in the middle of the room. The woolly mammoth, *Mammuthus primigenius*. The antithesis of prehistoric mammals, a four-tonne unit of thick, knotted brown fur and bone, raised on the trunks of its legs so that it stood almost four metres tall. Two thick, curved tusks exploded from its face, aimed toward the entrance of the exhibition hall so that anyone walking in was immediately greeted by the imposing silhouette of the beast; they were smooth and strong and burst from the thing's face like great curled trees, each one ending in a point sharp enough to smash through anything. The gigantic model was an abomination; more than that, it was a liability.

'What do we do?' said the last monk, a young Black man who hadn't yet spoken. He had lowered his hood, and his hair was closely-cropped but thick and curly. His eyes flashed fearfully in Andrea's direction; he was still gripping his knife tight by the handle. 'Just wait here?'

Andrea drew in a sharp breath. Turned to Rachel. The girl shrugged. For the first time Andrea saw that she was not afraid – or, at least, that her fright was not betrayed by her expression – and felt her admiration for the girl growing. She knew that Rachel had left her previous job to join the museum staff after one of her ex-colleagues had assaulted her; the young woman was far stronger than she let on. Sounded like she'd dealt with people far worse than any of these orange-robed psychopaths, and for as long as she'd worked here she'd never once mentioned it.

Andrea nodded confidently. 'Depends,' she said, turning back to the monk. Then she looked past him, glaring at Brother Arkham. 'Why would you want to control it?'

Fletcher and the blonde woman had made it to the back of the room and appeared from behind the central

147

display, moving to join them. The big monk wasn't grinning anymore, and his robes were spattered with blood.

Arkham sighed audibly, tearing his eyes from the moveless, roaring face of the mammoth. Shaking his head, he said, 'We don't answer to you.'

'It's powerful,' the blonde woman said bluntly. 'It's a source of power.'

'Sister Morgan...' warned Arkham, ducking beneath the tusk of the mammoth to move closer. 'I think that's enough.'

'It's definitely not,' Andrea snapped. 'What kind of power?'

Sister Morgan glanced at Arkham, then back again. 'When he was alive,' she said, ignoring the man's warning, 'he... the sorcerer... well, they thought he could raise the dead.'

'*Enough,*' Arkham said.

The woman swallowed. 'They thought he could raise the dead,' she echoed. 'They worshipped him for it.'

'They didn't just think it,' Arkham said briskly. 'You've seen it for yourself, now. He's up there—'

'Probably coming down here,' Rachel cut in.

'Yes, perhaps. Well, we'll be ready.'

'I'm sorry,' Andrea said, raising her hand. 'I'm still stuck on 'raising the dead'. Catch us up, here.'

Arkham's jaw set gravely. Glancing back toward

the foyer, he seemed to decide that they were safe for the moment, and nodded for the blonde woman to continue.

'There are different kinds of magic,' Sister Morgan said. 'His… chosen field, if you like… was necromancy. You've seen the paintings?'

Andrea nodded.

'Well, the people in those pictures – and the magician – were all part of some ancient cult. Or religion. Way back before the Aztecs, before the Ancient Egyptians. It's hard to say how wide they were spread, but… they're believed to have worshipped multiple gods. Some of them quite awful.'

'This power – the power to return the dead to life – was bestowed upon our magician by one of the gods of their order,' Arkham said. Over their heads, something heavy crashed against the roof with a *thwump*. It was moving across the floor above, stalking them.

'A nice one?' Rachel cut in sardonically.

'Oh, one of the friendliest, I'm sure,' Arkham smiled thinly. 'And, of course, the power went to his head – as one might imagine – and they lynched him. Figuratively speaking.'

'And the staff?'

'The staff – the *real* one'—with this he grimaced upward, his eyes flitting left to right to follow the sounds of movement above them—'was a measure of control. And the only thing that allowed his followers-cum-mutineers to stall him long enough that they could trap him in that sarcophagus.'

'And now you've let him out,' Andrea said.

'Imagine what we could *do* with that power,' Arkham said without hesitation, his eyes glittering brightly. They drilled into her, flashing cruelly in the deep, blue wash of the lights. 'You control the man, you control his gift. *Imagine.*'

'That's sick,' Rachel said disgustedly. There was another *thwump*, this time from the top of the stairs toward the end of the exhibition hall. She glanced at Sister Morgan. 'Can we have knives, too?'

'I'm guessing there's plenty of spares lying around upstairs,' Andrea murmured. Sister Morgan's eyes were fixed on the ceiling; the blonde woman pulled a brass chain from her robes, like the one that Andrea had glimpsed upstairs, and wound one end of it around her wrist. The other end dangled heavily past her waist, and a thick, round clamp – a shackle, Andrea supposed – glinted blue in the dim light. 'Not much good to us down here.'

Something moved in the lobby. A shadow flitted across the hall's arched entrance, a tall, lurching shadow in the shape of a man. Or something that looked vaguely like one.

'Take position,' Brother Arkham said quietly, and the monks braced themselves. Fletcher stepped up beside the yellow-robed man and spread his feet, bowing his body slightly as the shadow tilted back into the lobby. 'It's coming…'

The shape moved toward them suddenly. Andrea watched in horror as its head snapped around in their direction. The green glare of its eyes had gone, but she could almost smell the death reeking off it.

It lurched into the archway, a long, clawed shadow extending before it. Beside her, the dark-skinned monk gritted his teeth. Andrea's breath hitched in her throat.

The thing paused, just for a moment.

Then its whole body swayed forward and its face was illuminated by an explosion of soft blue as it burst out of the dark toward them.

Chapter 13

The mummy limped down a long, bleak corridor, flickering auxiliary lights above its head throwing dim orange candlelight onto the walls. Its body was bent and misshapen, one shoulder drooping so violently that it seemed to have been ripped from its socket. Strings of viscera hung off its bony hands, and a thick trail of red followed it along the stone flags, running into cracks and rivulets and painting a network of blood behind it. It dragged its feet, leaving ragged prints, its legs twisted like the angular legs of a predator bird.

The creature lurched through a narrow archway at the end of the corridor and into a wide, sparse gallery of paintings. Upon the walls canvases hung in incredible gold frames, smears of teal and black portraying stormy seas, scrawls and smudges of orange and thin seams of gold casting scenes into disarray: ancient warships ablaze, horizons bristling with lightning, great thrusting tentacles erupting from the deep.

The mummy paused in the middle of the room, doubled over as if breathing heavily. But its body contained no breath at all; it didn't blink, not once, and the shining green points of its eyes burned relentlessly in their sockets; it didn't salivate or shiver; in every respect, it was dead.

Didn't stop it, though.

The creature tipped its head back and its grinning maw fell open, smashed teeth separating like they'd been physically pulled apart. From the deep black hole within came another awful death rattle, a sound like roller skates juddering down a cobbled hill. The flakes of long-rotted flesh clinging to its skull bristled wetly, the ragged cloak strung around its neck fused to the sticky patches of decay between its shoulder-blades.

Its head snapped around suddenly and it lurched toward a door on the left, moving less like an injured rabbit and more like the lithe, preying creature which had dispatched the monks in the last room. It seemed to move fluidly and periodically between broken, dead thing and fearsome beast, one moment creaking and cracking as it hobbled and the next scuttling silently from floor to ceiling. It surged through the door into the dark of the next hall and moved through the museum like a wraith, completely soundless save for the rattle of its chest and the occasional *drip* of blood from its fingers.

Staggering out of a hall filled with stone figurines

and idols, the mummy lurched into another corridor and stopped again. It had crossed half the floor and could hear the faint sounds of life coming from somewhere below it; there would be a way down somewhere nearby. In fact…

Slowly it turned its head, looking toward the end of the corridor. Green fire blazed in its hollow eyes, the grin fused to its jaws widening impossibly. From here the stone floor seemed to fall away like a cliff, and beyond that it saw huge, distant walls slanting up toward the magnificent ceiling of the foyer.

Down there, voices echoed.

The mummy slopped a glossy red track along the corridor, moving with purpose, the ancient joints of its body crunching as they ground against each other. It flexed its fingers and the knuckles popped and cracked loudly, gold bangles slipping down the bony lengths of its forearms and clacking as they collided with the protruding bones of its wrists. The creature slunk like a wild dog, a narrow figure of gristle and anger that cast unnatural shadows on the walls as it passed by closed doors and unlit bulbs.

A door to the right had been left open and as it passed the creature's head swung round, its neck creaking dreadfully. A glassy kind of darkness existed through the doorway; twin points of green reflected back at the mummy from some distant screen.

Soft rattling sounds slipping through the gaps in its

bony maw, the mummy turned its whole body and stepped over the threshold.

The room was dark, but in the faint light from the corridor glass panes and cases were softly illuminated so that smears of greasy grey scattered the space immediately about the creature; moving toward the reflected spots of green it moved forward, dragging its feet, extending its hands into splayed, slender claws. Wary of the blazing points before it, ready to strike.

As it neared the glass cabinet in the centre of the room and triggered a tiny motion sensor, faint orange bulbs flickered to life around the edges of the ceiling. Glass pillars flooded suddenly with dim firelight, warm yellow halos outlining the silhouettes of broad, smooth-shouldered shapes.

Around the edges of the space, a series of wide stone sarcophagi had been stood so that the death masks and figures carved and painted upon them looked out into the middle of the room. There must have been a dozen of them, all ornately decorated with faded and peeling clots of blue and gold. A collection of Ancient Egyptian artefacts were stood on glass shelves between the standing sarcophagi, the possessions of those who had been buried within. Canopic jars lined the floor of many of the displays, some of them open. In one corner, a mummified cat stood attentive, its bandaged and decayed ears pricked up, its eyes covered by gauze, its whole body made thin and bony by age.

In the centre of the room, a single pillar of glass filled an enormous square space from floor to ceiling, a ring of softly-pulsing LEDs around its base pushing spotlights of yellow into a ring that flooded the display inside.

An open Egyptian sarcophagus stood at the back of the display, the gaping black pit of its carcass scraped and scarred by age. The lid was angled so that the blank blue eyes of the peaceful face carved into it were pointed into one corner of the room, the folded arms clutching two curved stone scimitars, arranged in a deadly cross over its chest.

The mummy had been removed from its coffin and stood at the front of the display, its face so close that it was almost pressed to the glass. Its body was slender, the legs bound together like the tail of a mermaid, the arms folded over its chest much as those of the stone figure on the face of its sarcophagus; its grinning skeletal jaw was exposed, a grey maw of gaps and cracked points, but otherwise the figure was completely wrapped in gauze. The bandages were grey-black and shone as though wet in the dim yellow glow of the LEDs. The eyeless mummy looked out toward the open doorway as if it were dreaming of escape.

The creature stepped toward the glass, a smeared reflection of its own decayed body aligning with the image of the Egyptian carcass behind the screen. For a moment their faces lined up almost perfectly, and the living mummy's green flaring eyes were superimposed on the blank mask of its Ancient Egyptian counterpart.

A shadow bent in the glass behind the shoulder of the creature's reflection. It froze.

Movement out in the corridor.

If the creature could have smiled with its awful gurning maw it might have. Something stirred in the shrivelled pit of the mummy's abdomen, a cruel yearning for flesh that translated to hunger by the time it surged up into the thing's sunken ribs. A heartless chest throbbed with longing and the creature clicked and rattled softly in anticipation.

A footstep in the corridor; the mummy withdrew into the darker corner of the room and scuttled along the glass, its body imbued again with the agile predator-like motions of a hunting animal. As a shadow fell across the doorway of the room the mummy's body straightened and, twisting in on itself, the thing scrambled up one of the glass cases and into the shelf of darkness above, burrowing into a thick wedge of pitch.

It watched the doorway with hungry green eyes as a frail silhouette stepped across the threshold.

The orange-robed woman could only have been in her early twenties. Her hood had been thrown back and her face was narrow and slight, dark hair tucked back behind her ears to reveal a single tattoo on each side of her neck: on the left, a crisp, black crescent moon, and on the right an ink-black circle which might have represented the sun. The mummy did not note her age, nor her storm-grey eyes; it only sensed the lifeblood pumping through her and thirsted for it. In life, the sorcerer had brought the dead back to their living; now, dead and millennia-old and finally free of the stone cage in which it had been trapped for so, *so* long, it was a rage-filled husk. The mummy understood nothing but hatred and hunger. The woman who had walked into the room was little more to it than another meal.

It crawled slowly across the top of the glass cases, watching as the woman stepped toward the central display. She gripped a familiar weapon in her hand: the staff, a long, smooth shaft of black that exploded at its point into a head of ragged bone. And there, inside, the green jewel, flickering as it caught the light.

Her eyes flitted to the floor; she could see the smears of blood where the creature had stood, and the track of plump, red drops it had left as it skittered across the room. Slowly, she began to follow the trail.

The creature stalked her from above, moving back toward the door as she delved into the shadows.

'I know you're in here, you undead fuck,' she called.

She paused at the glass, swallowing hard as she saw the thick, dark smear of viscera where the creature had pressed its back to the screen. Behind it, the blank face of one of the many sarcophagi stared out at her.

The creature crouched above the doorway, pinned to the ceiling, tiny points of death glinting in the deep pits of its face. Slowly, it reached out a bony hand and twisted its wrist.

Silently it snatched its fingers into a fist. Green sparks crackled around the edges of its eye-sockets, ragged seams of lightning flaring briefly as tiny flecks of light danced around its skeletal hand, embers dashing the faded gold bangle on its wrist.

The woman shuddered suddenly as the air bristled with energy.

'All right,' she said, backing toward the door – towards the mummy – and raising the spear. 'Come out, then, let's see what else you got.'

In the corner of the room, one of the sarcophagi suddenly wobbled.

The woman whirled round, thrusting the spear in the direction of the sound. 'What the…'

Another started to move, shuddering behind the glass, and her eyes went wide. Something moaned, its awful voice muffled through the stone of another sarcophagus. The other side of the room, something began to pound at the granite from within.

In the centre of the exhibit, the bandaged mummy behind the glass began to twitch on the iron rods holding it up. Flecks of dust were sprayed from its chest as its arms strained against their bonds. Its mouth hung slack and its head rolled stiffly. The woman screamed, backing up toward the corridor.

When she was directly underneath the creature, it pounced.

It fell through the air and leapt onto her back, a mangled clot of bone which enveloped the woman's shoulders and slammed her into the floor, clawing and biting. The woman shrieked and crawled out of its grip, her cheek cut into bloody ribbons, somehow still gripping the staff. All around them the corpses trapped in their sarcophagi slammed bandaged fists on the stone, filling the glass cases with a massive echoing soundscape that sounded like rain repeatedly smacking the churning surface of a river, or like artillery fire.

'You old dead son of a bitch!' the woman yelled, scrambling to her feet and pointing the glittering head of the spear in the mummy's direction. 'Fuck you, Skeletor!'

She rushed forward and swung the spear like a baseball bat. The bony head of the thing crashed into the mummy's skull and there was a sick, resounding *crack*.

The mummy stumbled, and for a moment everything was silent. Its skull was tilted forward, the green lights in its eyes extinguished. It wobbled, its whole body suddenly seeming very small and shrivelled.

The woman swung the spear again with a yell.

The mummy's head shot up, its eyes flashing emerald, and it lunged at her, batting the staff from her hands as a rapture of noise exploded all around them, slamming and banging and moaning muffled by stone but loud enough to drown out the pounding of blood in her ears—

The last thing the woman saw before darkness consumed her and a hot, red sensation spread across her belly was the mummy's face, inches from hers, a mask of bone that was so ferocious and animalistic that it looked like the face of the devil.

'Bruce!' Andrea hissed, bolting across the hall toward the lurching figure in the archway. 'What the hell are you doing here?'

She rushed at him, glancing into the shadows of the foyer before wrapping him in a tight hug. Bruce swayed on his heels as she squeezed his body, never more pleased to see him than right now. Somewhere in the room, Rachel exhaled a sharp breath of relief; upstairs, something skittered across the smooth stone floor of another exhibition hall.

'Oh, thank god you're here,' she whispered, running her hand up his back as she pressed her head into his chest. Arkham and the others stayed back, apparently no longer concerned with keeping her restrained; it was possible they had more pressing matters to worry themselves with. Or that they had realised she'd be utterly stupid to run into the belly of the museum without some form of protection. Or...

She pulled back suddenly, gripping Bruce's arms. 'Why *are* you here?' she said calmly.

Bruce shook his head. He looked bewildered, but otherwise unharmed, still dressed in his work clothes. He smelled faintly of floral perfume and for the briefest fraction of a second Andrea felt more insecure than she ever had; she had never been the type to succumb too easily to jealousy, but this was not the first occasion that Bruce had given her a reason to be vaguely doubtful.

It wasn't that that made her skin crawl, though. It was the blank look on his face, and the sick whisper in her mind, a reminder of Brother Arkham's words from earlier: *Don't you know?* he'd said when she'd asked how they had known about the staff. *Your* friend *told us.*

'Bruce,' she whispered, taking a step back. 'Please tell me you didn't...'

Bruce looked from her to the mammoth, his gaze pinned on the tangled mass of fur obscuring its face for a moment before he looked past them both, to the monks and Rachel.

'Oh, god,' she breathed, clamping a hand over her mouth. It all made sense. Perfect, horrifying sense.

'You did, didn't you? That's why you never seemed interested in my work – you were covering yourself. Why would you do this, Bruce? What the hell is wrong with—'

'Woman, what the fuck are you on about?' Bruce snapped suddenly, his eyes flitting back to hers. 'Jesus Christ, shut up for a second, would you? The moment I step in the door there's screaming everywhere, and then I come down here and find you playing silly buggers with a bunch of monks – what is this, some kind of escape room bollocks? A toga party?'

Andrea frowned. 'I… what? Bruce, you're not—'

'No,' he shook his head, raising both hands as though trying to distance himself from her. 'Whatever you're about to say, the answer's probably *no*.'

'What are you doing here?' she said.

Bruce raised an eyebrow. 'I came here to apologise, believe it or not. But since you're clearly *preoccupied*, forget it. I'll let you get back to your weird party, shall I?'

He turned to step out of the Hall of Pleistocene Mammals and Andrea lurched forward, grabbing him by the arm. 'No, you can't go out there,' she said, looking desperately back at the monks as if they might offer her some support. 'It's dangerous, there's something – a creature—'

'Oh, piss off,' Bruce said, shrugging her off and stepping backward. 'I've had enough of you, to be honest, love. You're so fucking high maintenance I may as well be working two full-time jobs, you know?'

He threw another look into the hall and grimaced.

'And your friends are weird as shit. What, do the men in skirts take you and the Black girl and do shit to you in the dark? D'you like that, huh?'

'*What?!*' Andrea seethed, almost forgetting the mummy was somewhere in the building.

'Never mind. Clearly I picked a bad time of the month to think I could deal with you rationally,' Bruce said bitterly.

Andrea blinked.

'What's that look for, hm?' he jeered. 'Get a grip, Andy, this was never going to work. You're too... selfish.'

'Oh, god,' Andrea said quietly. 'It *does* make sense. All of it.'

'Excuse me?'

She shook her head, stepping back. The shadow of the mammoth's looming tusk fell over her. 'You're just a cunt, aren't you?'

Bruce's mouth opened.

'Fuck off, then,' she said, 'go back out there, get yourself killed. See if I care, you outrageous prick of a man.'

'I'm sorry?'

'We're done, dickhead,' she shook her head, stepping back again. 'I'll take my chances with the

Brotherhood of Tasteless Robes, thank you.'

'Fine,' Bruce said. 'I was done, anyway. Fuck you.'

'Fuck *you*,' Andrea said, retreating into the dark. She realised, suddenly, that her fingers felt completely fine, that if she flexed them at the knuckles they bent freely. Clarity seemed to flow through her, calm and sweet, and she felt freer than she had for a long time.

Bruce smirked. 'All right. It's not like I've not got options, you—'

His face twisted in agony as something thrust out of his chest, forcing a thick jet of viscera from between his ribs. Bruce staggered, his back blown forward by the impact of whatever had slammed into him, and suddenly Andrea noticed a second silhouette behind his, slightly shorter, slightly broader, its elbows bent as though it was gripping him by the spine. Her breath hitched and she rushed forward, her eyes dropping from Bruce's confused, slightly-bemused expression to the thick, glossy shaft of metal poking out of his torso.

'Oh god,' Andrea moaned, lunging forward to catch him as the blade slid out of his back and he crumpled to his knees, another spurt of blood and ichor exploding from his chest. More dribbled down his chin and she realised he was drooling thick gobs of crimson, his eyes rolling lazily as his head bobbed forward. She dug her hands into his armpits and grunted as the weight of his upper body flopped limply onto her, warm blood instantly soaking her clothes. 'Oh, god, Bruce, no…'

She looked up, past him, and her eyes went wide with a sickening realisation.

Dr Melvin Phillips stood above Bruce's kneeling, convulsing body, his face flat and emotionless, his eyes dark and menacing. He gripped a Roman gladius in one hand, a stubby double-edged steel blade drooling with blood, and his free hand was bunched into a tight, knotted fist, trembling with adrenaline. The portly old man was splashed with red and the soft blue lights of the exhibition hall glinted in the whites of his eyes.

Bruce suddenly went very, very still in Andrea's arms. 'No…' she moaned, running splayed fingers over his back in search of a wound to press or to plug. Blood bubbled through her fingers and gushed from the hole in his spine and she sobbed madly, her whole body shuddering as his corpse stiffened and stopped writhing.

Gently as she could, she staggered back and lowered him gently to the floor. Anger pulsed through her, anger and confusion and cold, thick rage. Covered in blood, she glared at Phillips and gritted her teeth.

'You,' she whispered.

He smiled. 'Sorry, old friend.'

***

'I don't believe it,' Andrea said, her eyes stinging with tears, 'How could you?'

Phillips stared blankly at her.

'How *could* you?!'

He shrugged. Accusingly, he said, 'Your mother's going to lay me off. All of us, eventually. I have my connections. I knew they were looking for the staff, and I knew you had your eye on it too. When I sent you that e-mail, I called Mr Arkham, too. He made me an offer.'

'You sold me out for *money*?' Andrea said. 'People have died, Mel. Darren, the caretaker – they killed him! And that creature…'

Phillips looked from the soaked gladius in his hand to Bruce's still body, and then back to Andrea. 'Your point?' he said flatly.

'Do you even know what they're going to do with this thing? What they'd be capable of?'

'It was a very generous offer,' Phillips said quietly.

'You still think you're getting paid?' Brother Arkham spat, storming forward. He stepped over the body on the floor and poked Phillips in the chest, spittle flying as he spoke. 'The staff was fake. You understand? The staff was a fucking fake.'

'Well, then,' Phillips said, 'there's nothing to be done with the creature except kill it or trap it until you find the real thing.'

'If we kill it, we lose everything,' the monk shook

his head.

'Who cares?' Andrea cried. 'Kill the fucking thing before it slaughters us all! What happens when it's done in the building, hm? When it gets bored of the paintings and decides to take a walk outside?'

'Oh, shut up,' Phillips groaned childishly. Turning back to Arkham, he gripped the sword tight and thrust it forward. 'I was promised a certain sum. And you're going to make sure that money is transferred to me, real staff or not. The information I gave you was genuine. The risks I took were real. I deserve what I was promised.'

'What you were promised came with conditions,' Brother Arkham snapped.

'I agree with Baldy,' Rachel called, stepping out of the shadow of the *Megatheriidae*. 'You sold them dodgy goods, you don't get your money.'

Phillips looked from Rachel to Andrea. His expression softened for a moment. She thought she might have caught a flash of regret in his eye; but then it was gone, and his jaw hardened again. 'You let her be a part of this?' he said quietly. 'You irresponsible—'

'Well, I didn't know you'd arranged this lovely surprise, did I?' Andrea said sardonically.

'You want your money,' Brother Arkham said, 'you'll stay with us and help us trap it.'

'We're not going to kill it?' Rachel said.

The monk turned to her and grimaced. 'It's useless to us dead. If we kill it, we lose everything we've worked toward. Everything we *are*. We're going to put it back in the box, and when we find the real staff, we're going to have it under our control.'

'Uh-uh,' Phillips said. 'I only came to make sure everything was going smoothly. You can handle this without me, boys.'

He glanced to the back of the room, nodded curtly in Sister Morgan's direction.

'Boys and girls. Apologies.'

Briskly he lowered the sword and stepped back, glancing up as he moved into the half-light of the lobby. Above them, something scuttled across the stone walls. Phillips faltered, stepping forward again – and Brother Arkham grabbed him by the shirt, yanking him back into the hall.

'You will stay,' he whispered, and Andrea's eye was drawn down by a flash of silver. Arkham had a blade pinned to Phillips' stomach. 'You will stay until it is trapped, or you are dead.'

Phillips smiled weakly. 'Fine,' he said. He looked at Rachel. 'One last project together before we're all downsized, eh?'

'Fuck yourself,' Rachel said.

Andrea cocked an eyebrow in surprise. It might just have been the first time she'd heard the younger woman swear.

'Well, if that's how it's going to be,' Phillips murmured, withdrawing himself from the yellow-robed monk's grip and stepping past the mammoth's tusk to join Andrea in the shadows. 'Let's get this bollocks over with, shall we?'

Chapter 14

The boy had practiced for hours, but nothing had come of it.

Nothing ever did.

He was small, shrew-like, sunken into himself. Nine years old, with small ash-white patches in his cropped, brown hair; though treatment had brought most of his hair back over the last eight months, he knew that his father expected his condition to progress to alopecia *totalis* within a few years. His skin was pale, his eyes a piercing blue. Some days he looked like death.

A knock on his bedroom door jolted him from his half-hearted efforts and he bolted upright at his desk. The room was small, mostly overtaken by a single bed with a Thomas the Tank Engine bedspread. On a pine bedside cabinet, a stack of books stood beside a stubby, mushroom-shaped lamp; tabs of pills lay spread about the base of the lamp, some of which had been arranged in a plastic blue pillbox.

The door pressed open gently and Megan stepped in, moving softly over the thin carpet as though afraid to disturb something. She smiled at her brother and he smiled sadly back. There was something clutched tightly in both of her hands; her fingers were open slightly, but the boy couldn't see what might be in the dark pit of her palms. It seemed to be wriggling.

'No luck?' Megan said, glancing toward the desk at which her brother sat.

The boy shook his head, returning his attention to the thing on his desk. He sat in a black office chair that was far too big for him, the back straight and tall and uncomfortable. Gripping both the plastic arms of the chair, he sighed. 'He's going to kill me.'

His voice was strained and bent with an odd, repressive weight.

Megan stepped over to the desk and paused. 'I have an idea,' she said.

Outside, the crunch of tyres over the gravel driveway and the soft, gentle stall of the engine.

'Please,' the boy said, 'don't... don't try anything. He'll know. He always knows.'

'He won't.'

Below them the car door slammed shut and they heard their father's footsteps crunching toward the front door. 'He'll know,' the boy whispered.

On the desk, a small iron-barred hamster cage sat

174

surrounded by papers and drawings and diagrams. The papers were yellowed and torn at the edges, scrawled upon with black ink; the drawings were obscene. Inside the cage, on a bed of pale sawdust, lay the still, small body of a dead white mouse. It was on its back, its tiny feet curled into claws, its head tipped back, eyes blank.

He had been staring at it almost exclusively since his father had left for work.

'Here, just let me,' his sister said, folding the thing she had brought into one hand and reaching for the latch of the cage's barred door. 'It might get him off your back. Just for a little bit.'

The boy winced. His father expected enough of him as it was. 'Please...'

But Megan had already opened the cage door and, with one hand, scooped the tiny plump carcass out of the box. Quickly she laid it on the desk and, glancing one more time at the boy, replaced it with the thing in her hand. From downstairs the muffled sounds of conversation floated up through the floorboards; the boy's parents would only indulge in a quick catch-up before he came upstairs to see what progress had been made.

Megan closed the cage door and retreated, swiping the tiny body from the desk. 'There,' she said, 'just see if this doesn't make him happy, at least for a little while.'

She planted a kiss on the back of the boy's head and moved swiftly across the room, avoiding all the spots where the floorboards creaked. Her brother stared at the thing inside the cage, afraid that his father would see through the ruse, afraid of what might happen if he did.

'Good luck,' Megan said in the doorway, and then she disappeared onto the landing and headed quietly back to her room.

Moments after the boy's bedroom door had shut, he heard footsteps approaching up the stairs. 'Miles?' his father called as he moved onto the landing, the boards groaning beneath his feet. 'How's it going in there, buddy?'

The boy didn't answer. He just stared wide-eyed at the thing in the cage and swallowed hard.

A sharp, loud knock, and before Miles' heart had stopped pounding the door swung wide open and his father breezed in. 'All right,' he started, 'let's see how you've—'

The man froze in the middle of the room. Still with his back to the door, Miles squeezed his eyes shut. This was wrong, it would never work, he would *know*...

'My god, boy, you've done it,' his father breathed.

Suddenly he was at the boy's shoulder, leaning down to peer into the cage.

'Dear *god*...'

Miles' father was not the kind of man who was

176

easily impressed. He was tall, broad-shouldered, with thick brown hair and a moustache that screamed 1930s capitalist. His stubbled jaw was square and firm, his eyes dark; he always reminded Miles of a circus ringmaster in a mustard yellow shirt and brown jacket, an imposing beast of a man who chewed cigars and spoke like there was one in his mouth at all times.

He clapped Miles on the back and laughed softly. 'You've done it,' he echoed. 'You've finally done it.'

Inside the cage, a tiny white mouse darted from one end of its sawdust bed to the other, still warm from being clutched in Megan's palms. Its fur was bright and healthy, its belly bloated and its eyes gleaming with life.

Miles exhaled shallow, anxious breaths and opened his eyes, glancing up. His father wasn't looking at him, but focused entirely on the mouse. 'Harriet!' he yelled suddenly. 'The boy's done it!'

Suddenly Miles' father turned to the boy, grinning down at him from beneath that dark, well-oiled moustache. His teeth flashed hungrily as he knelt on the floor, gripping the child's arms.

'Do you know how long I've waited for this?' Miles' father whispered.

Miles nodded.

'Oh, my boy… I'm so proud of you,' the man said, squeezing tightly. 'This gift – passed down through our family, generation to generation to generation – and oh, what a gift it is… I am so, *so proud.*'

He leaned in and squeezed the boy in a constricting hug. Miles winced as the bruises on his back burned with pain. 'Dad, I—'

'Shh,' the man whispered. 'You must be exhausted. Oh, I'm so happy. I shall run downstairs and telephone your grandfather in a minute. He'll be very pleased. You know, the strength that you have – the power to raise the dead – do you know the things you could do with that power?'

Miles shook his head.

His father leaned back again, still squeezing the boy's arms. 'You know, your ancestor – many thousands of years ago, boy – your ancestor did great things with his gift. See, it was given to him by the gods, and he knew that could only mean that it was meant for greatness. That *he* was meant for greatness.'

Miles had heard this story many times. Had heard that the sorcerer who was first bestowed with this 'gift' had died before he'd known his mistress was pregnant, that he'd passed on the power through blood. That he'd been *killed.*

'We shall talk more in a moment,' Miles' father said, standing straight and pinching the boy's cheek. 'I must tell your grandfather before—'

In her bedroom, Megan screamed.

Miles' whole body went cold at the sound as he realised – almost immediately, but an eternity too late

– what was about to happen.

'What the…' his father murmured, rushing out of the room.

'No,' Miles whispered, flopping out of the chair and staggering across his room, moving without thinking, already knowing what he'd see when he looked out into the corridor.

Nonetheless, he looked.

Miles' father stood in the doorway of Megan's bedroom across the landing, looming over the girl. His shadow was an enormous bank of darkness and he rose from it like a mountain, filling all the space that Miles could see.

'That little monster put this awful thing in my bed!' Megan sobbed, holding something aloft, presenting it to her father like a trophy. Miles didn't have to look into her hands to know what the thing was.

His heart sunk, seemed to stop beating altogether, as his father slowly turned to look in his direction. His eyes were like thunder.

Behind him, Megan grinned wickedly.

'You despicable little brat,' Miles' father said, storming across the landing. Already reaching for his belt, he barrelled into the boy's room as the boy retreated into the corner. Fumbling with the buckle, he yelled, 'You ungrateful, childish little fucker! To think – oh, to think, boy – I was so *proud*…'

The belt came off, slithering from its loops like a

black snake from its nest, coiled and ready to strike, and the bruises and welts on Miles' back and ribs seemed to cry out all at once in recognition.

'No,' Miles wailed, 'please, it wasn't... I didn't...'

Atop the boy's desk, the caged mouse watched uninterestedly as Miles Arkham's quivering form disappeared beneath the mountainous silhouette of his father and a rage that was thousands of years old.

Brother Arkham stood with Andrea in the shadows of the great still mammoth, both of them watching the archway into the foyer. Two of Arkham's monks guarded the opening: Brother Fletcher stood on the left, his back to the wall, a long, heavy-looking chain gripped in both hands and hanging past his knees; on the right, the dark-skinned monk who Andrea had learned was called Brother Cowey stood holding something that resembled a snare pole – the sort of thing you might use to catch an alligator by the neck, or, she thought, whack an ancient mummy round the back of the head from a distance of about four or five feet. Somewhere in the dark the other side of the mammoth, Sister Morgan stood brandishing a pair of knives.

Andrea couldn't rip her eyes away from Bruce's body. It lay in the archway where it had fallen, blood pooling around its midsection, its arm bent at an awkward angle so that its fingers clutched uselessly at the air. A pang of guilt stung her, knifed right through her stomach. The last things she'd said to him had been cruel. Well deserved, but cruel nonetheless, and bitter. Hateful. She wished she could take them back – no, not entirely, in fact not at all, but she wished he hadn't *died* right after she'd said them – wished that they hadn't been the *last things he'd heard* before the gladius ruptured his lungs and crashed through his ribs.

Dr Melvin Phillips stood at the very back of the room, holding the brutish little sword with one hand, the other curled into a tight fist by his side.

Bruce's body looked so small from back here. Washed in the soft blue light, stiff and moveless... peaceful. God, she would have to tell his mother. Oh, god. Christ.

A hand slipped into hers and squeezed. She looked round, her eyes meeting Rachel's. the young woman stood beside her, a comforting presence amongst all this. Andrea had dragged her into this. Had been stupid enough to put her in danger. And the girl had hardly complained at all, despite everything. She'd been more resilient than any of them.

'I'm sure he knew how you really felt about him,' Rachel whispered, somehow reading her mind.

Andrea swallowed, her eyes returning to the corpse twenty feet from where they stood. 'That *was* how I really felt about him,' she said quietly. 'I just wish I hadn't realised that two minutes before he…'

Nearby, Brother Arkham stiffened. 'Quiet,' he said.

Ignoring him, Rachel said, 'You know, I had a girlfriend in college who was just like him. She was arrogant, rude… I don't think she was into girls, even, just wanted to see what it was like. She used me. I didn't see it at the time, I was… well, I suppose I was in love. I told her everything private, everything secret that I'd never told anyone before, because I felt like I could trust her. Then—'

'Enough,' Arkham whispered, shooting them a look. There was something in his hand, Andrea saw, something that he had withdrawn from his belt, something that didn't look much like a knife.

'She was one of the popular girls, see,' Rachel said, keeping her voice way down, 'and when I sort of found out what she was really like… well, it turned out she'd been telling all her friends about me. Feeding them every little detail – all the things I'd told her; all the things we had done together; all the little mistakes I made in the bedroom, every one of them – and they *loved* it. And I got angry, and I said some awful things to her. Truly awful things.'

Above them, something scuttled from one wall to another, its animal-like movements muffled through the stone. That's it, Andrea thought, that's the mummy, it's coming. Either side of the archway, Brother Fletcher and Brother Cowey stiffened.

'Two weeks later, she was hit by a bus. Ended up in hospital for six months,' Rachel said. 'I can't say I was even very upset, not really. I was so full of hate for her, I… you know. I wouldn't have wished it on her, not for all the world, but once I knew she was going to be okay I kind of just got on my life. But everyone simpered over her, and cried over her – and everyone in all my classes kind of drifted away from me – and I realised… you know, what if it *was* my fault? In some twisted way, what if *I* did this?'

'It wasn't…' Andrea started. Rachel squeezed her hand.

'No,' she said. 'Exactly. It wasn't. Two completely unrelated things happened. Correlation or causation, right? Or something like that. I wasn't driving the bus. And you and him… it sounded like what you said had been coming for a long time. But you didn't stick a sword in him.'

'No,' Andrea said softly, glancing back toward Phillips, who stood quivering behind them. 'I didn't. And when we're out of here, I'm going to kill the fucker who did.'

Phillips swallowed.

'I'm so sorry,' Rachel said. 'I'm so sorry for what happened to him. And what's happening here. I—'

'It's not your fault,' Andrea shook her head. 'None of it. And I'm sorry you're here, I should have sent you home. If not before, then the moment they all showed

183

up, I should have got you out of here.'

'Ah, you'd be lost without me,' Rachel said.

The two of them stood together in the dark, weaponless and terrified, surrounded by men who didn't care if they lived through the next ten minutes. Wrong place at the wrong time, Andrea thought, but it didn't matter. None of it mattered.

'I think I'm going to be sick,' she whispered, and then something shattered in the foyer.

Her heart smacked her ribcage and Rachel gripped her hand even tighter, crushing the life out of her knuckles. A dark, grey smudge appeared the other side of the lobby, halfway up the wall, clinging to the stonework with bony hands and the sharpened nubs of its toes. It glanced once in their direction, head tipping back, eyes flaring green. Then it lunged across the lobby, scaling the wall like some remote-control spider on a velodrome, and disappeared out of sight.

'Be ready,' Arkham whispered softly.

'We might be if you'd give us a damn knife between us,' Andrea hissed.

Rachel shook her head. 'I'm scared,' she said.

'I know,' Andrea said, squeezing her hand tight. 'Me too. But we're getting out of here. It's going to be okay.'

'You don't know what the fuck you're talking about,' Phillips said behind them.

'Shut up,' Rachel said.

Light thudding sounds rang through the foyer as the creature skittered over the ceiling. Faded again as it passed across the archway. Andrea drew in a breath and held it. Beside the opening, Brother Fletcher looked in Sister Morgan's direction and nodded, mouthing something indiscernible. Andrea heard the woman sobbing gently from the other side of the mammoth's bulk..

They were all going to die in here.

Gently, Andrea let go of Rachel's hand. The younger woman looked at her, terrified, but Andrea shook her head before the girl could say anything. Wordlessly, Andrea nodded discretely in Phillips' direction.

After a moment, Rachel nodded back.

Her head snapped back to the archway as a shadow fell over Bruce's body. For a moment she didn't see anything, then she realised that the shape of the archway itself had changed, a stony lump appearing at the top; the mummy clung to the wall above the arch, leering in through the opening. Its green eyes flashed and it grinned.

'Here we go,' said Phillips.

'Now,' Andrea hissed, lurching back and slamming the weight of her whole body into him, bringing an elbow crashing up into his nose. Phillips squawked, tumbling back into the wall, his grip loosening momentarily. Rachel darted for the gladius and grabbed it by the handle before it could clatter to the floor, rolling onto her side with the weight of the thing.

In the archway, the mummy dropped to the floor, an angular strip of darkness separating from the shadows above.

It stood on two feet, one shoulder dipped low, its slender bony arms hanging by its sides. The rags of its cloak made its silhouetted upper body bulky and ragged, its midsection caved in, its legs stripped of all their flesh. Its skull was a mangled dome of carbon that might as well have been fossilised, the only life among its deep pits and cracks the twin fires in its eye-sockets. Its grin was an awful smashed mess of teeth.

'You broke my nose, you bitch,' Phillips hissed, clamping a hand over his face as blood streamed down into his mouth. Rachel stumbled away from him, the sword in both hands, and Andrea moved to join her, turning her head toward the archway as the mummy stepped forward.

'Now!' Brother Arkham yelled, and the monks at the archway lunged forward. Brother Cowey swung the snare pole, smacking the back of the mummy's head hard before snatching the weapon back. The mummy wheeled around, snarling loudly, swinging with a clawed, grey hand. Cowey ducked the blow and thrust the snare pole into the creature's throat; it stumbled back and Brother Fletcher staggered clumsily forward, swinging the long, iron chain in his hands like a lasso. The blunt weight of the iron smashed into the mummy's ribs and knocked it to its knees.

For a moment, it looked like they were winning.

'Look out!' Rachel yelled suddenly. Andrea snapped her head back to see Phillips coming at her, his teeth bared, one hand clutching at his nose while the other knotted into a fat-fingered fist and snaked back over his shoulder. She ducked as he launched his arm forward, narrowly avoiding his knuckles. He tipped forward, following through with the blow, and she staggered back as he rocked unsteadily on his feet, already whirling back toward her.

In the archway the monk with the snare pole had managed to snap the noose around the mummy's neck and he was struggling with it as the creature struggled, snapping and biting and clawing at him. Fletcher came at the monk again, the chain pulled tight as if he meant to garrotte the creature, but the thing launched an elbow back into his throat and Fletcher staggered into the wall and slumped.

'Fuck off!' Andrea snapped, kicking out blindly in the vague direction of Phillips' stomach. Her toe connected with something soft and he grunted, doubling over. Thrusting her heel forward she ploughed it into his shoulder and knocked him back; Phillips stumbled into the central display, the back of his head loudly thwacking the mammoth's leg. Rachel swung the sword toward him, held the point of the blade inches from his throat.

'Stay down,' she said. Phillips nodded sharply, one hand still pressed to his cracked nose.

'I can't hold it!' yelled Brother Cowey.

Andrea looked. Before her, Brother Arkham was frozen stiff, glued to the floor. Brother Fletcher gasped, his back pressed to the wall, winded and trying desperately to suck oxygen in his lungs.

Brother Cowey held the snare pole at arm's length, the snarling creature caught up in the cables of the noose and swiping furiously at the air. They swung around in a mad dance: something that might have looked funny if not for the absolute terror in Cowey's eyes and the glistening strings of blood drooling from the mummy's jaw.

'Leave him alone!' Sister Morgan yelled, bursting forward suddenly, both knives gripped tightly in her hands. She ducked beneath a swiping arm and jammed one of the blades hard into the creature's side, withdrawing her body from its reach as the knife stuck. The thing roared, its bright green eyes darting down to the handle of the thing poking out of its ribs.

Beside Andrea, Rachel stood quivering, her eyes on the horror in the archway, her hand pressing the sword firmly into Phillips' chest.

Her bravery ignited by the success of the first swing, Sister Morgan lurched at the mummy again, swinging the second into its stony face.

The mummy reacted faster than Andrea could have imagined, thrusting one arm back to grab Morgan's wrist then, in the same fluid motion, twisting its whole body around and clenching its bony fingers around the blade of the knife. Morgan squeezed as the hand gripping her wrist tightened, bones crunching in her arm; the knife slid from her fingers as they straightened helplessly. The wire noose glinted around the mummy's knife as Cowey tried to yank the creature back; too late.

The knife twisted in its skeletal hand and plunged into Morgan's eye-socket, burrowing immediately into her brain. She slumped to the floor.

'No!' Andrea yelled, rushing forward. Brother Arkham turned, extending an arm to grab her by the arm. She struggled against him but he was strong, holding her back, almost shoving her behind him.

Brother Fletcher lurched forward, swinging the chains into the mummy's stomach. There was a dreadful crunch as the weapon exploded into bone and he whipped the chains back, screaming loudly as he snapped them into the thing's neck, then its thigh, then into its gut again.

The mummy screeched and slammed its head forward, pulling Brother Cowey and the snare pole with it as it slammed the bone into Fletcher's nose. Fletcher staggered. Before Andrea could blink the creature had turned and then it was clawing at the noose around its neck, curling its bony fingers around the cable and yanking hard, its head twisting and growling all the while. Helplessly Andrea watched as the noose snapped. The mummy roared triumphantly, leaping forward – pouncing – and barrelling into Cowey's chest. The man crashed into the wall behind him and the prehistoric beasts in the display shuddered with the impact.

Andrea screamed again as the mummy bore down on Cowey's convulsing body, biting savagely into his throat. Blood exploded across its face.

'Enough!' Fletcher yelled, suddenly behind the creature. He swung the chains high and looped them quickly around the creature's neck, crossing his arms and yanking it onto its feet. The mummy roared, bellowed from deep within its gut, then staggered forward, heading for the mammoth, for *them*—

Brother Arkham stepped forward, raising his arm, and Andrea finally saw the thing in his hand.

A loud *crack!* of thunder echoed all through the museum as he squeezed the trigger and the gun exploded.

'Get back!' Andrea yelled. 'Get back, you're going to fucking die!'

Arkham ignored her, firing off another shot. A third smacked the creature's chest, another its shoulder, every impact sending a cloud of grey dust into the air and knocking the creature back a pace. Five—

Brother Fletcher staggered back as a bullet punched a deep, black hole between his eyes, throwing him across the room. Rachel yelled in shock but Arkham kept pushing forward, pointing the barrel right at the creature's heart. The chain clattered loudly onto the floor and the mummy lurched forward, taking long hungry strides, completely unfazed. Angrier than ever, thick gobs of blood flying from its mouth as it roared.

Suddenly Arkham swung down, pointing the gun at the creature's knee. He squeezed the trigger again and another explosion rang across the room as thick clumps of ichor were punched from the mummy's leg. It screeched, slumping onto one knee, and Arkham marched forward, slamming the barrel into the thing's bony skull. 'Die,' he whispered.

'No, get bac—"

Click.

The mummy thrust both hands upward in a smeared, bloody arc and smashed them into Arkham's chest, plunging them deep and ripping them out again in a ragged streak of movement. It bellowed horribly as it squeezed something wet and pulsing in one hand, then cast it aside, bored of it.

It seemed to laugh as Arkham fell to the floor, his chest open, his eyes wide and staring.

The man's heart lay throbbing beside Bruce's body, slippery and red. Slowly, almost gently, it stopped.

Andrea took a step back.

The mummy swung its body forward and glared at her, grinning hungrily, its face splashed with red.

Chapter 15

Rachel screamed, raising the sword with both hands as the mummy lurched to its feet and slogged toward them. Its shot knee buckled as it walked, spouts of dust puffing out of thick funnelled holes in its chest and skull. The green points of its eyes flickered weakly.

They were all that was left, Andrea realised.

'What do we do?' Rachel yelled. 'What the hell do we do?'

Andrea wheeled around, looking down as something moved at the edge of her vision. Phillips stumbled to his feet, both his hands raised in surrender, looking between them as he straightened. Then he looked in the direction of the creature and balked.

Andrea swallowed.

'I'm gone,' Phillips muttered, backing away. The mummy was approaching their little corner of the room, moving fast on its shattered knee, snarling hungrily as it reached out for them.

Andrea shook her head as Phillips staggered around

the back of the mammoth and moved around the other side of its bulky, massive frame, moving clumsily toward the archway.

'You fucker!' Rachel yelled, but already he was gone, disappearing into the foyer. His running footsteps echoed softly as he pelted up the stairs.

Andrea backed up as the mummy closed in on them, its grinning skull lit a soft, pale blue. Its bony arms snapped back and it flexed its fingers, clutching them into sharp, knotted claws, twisting them in the air. Little more than a grey skeleton in rags, it opened its maw and that awful, low death rattle rolled wetly up its throat.

'Stay back,' Andrea said flatly, and all at once she lurched forward and bolted past the mummy. She bumped its shoulder as she passed, felt claws scrape the flesh of her cheek and draw blood, stumbled forward—

'What are you doing?' Rachel yelled as Andrea ran forward, heels slipping in the blood splashed across the floor. The mummy had whirled around and it was coming after her already, the dreadful clicking of its feet on the hard stone echoing in her ears. She ducked under the thick, curved tusk of the mammoth, its enormous shaggy trunk looming long and looping above her. She dived for the nearest body and grabbed at the chains that had fallen near it, cringing as the cold iron seared her palms. Turning fast, she dipped her head back with a yell as the skeletal creature clawed at her face.

Staggering back, her shin bumped something soft and she gasped sharply, repulsed by the feel of dead flesh against her leg. The mummy lunged forward and she let the chain slip into one hand, throwing it back and swinging—

The length of the chain whacked the mummy's neck hard and the snaking tail of the thing snapped around, forming an angular metal scarf around its throat with a dry *crunch*.

'Ha!' Andrea yelled, yanking her arm back and twisting her body around the mummy as it swiped at her again. She had it on a leash now, another length of chain swinging about its waist from the collar she'd looped around its neck.

What the fuck next?

She screamed as the mummy thrust a hand forward and caught her in the ribs, tipping her head back in pain, hair falling out of her eyes. She met the dull, blank gaze of the mammoth, its own glassy eyes half-hidden beneath the mess of fur covering its face. 'You'll do,' she whispered breathlessly.

Grinning, she stumbled past the mummy again, dragging it with the chain around its neck. 'Rachel, bring that thing over here!' she yelled, ploughing forward as the creature tried to pull her back, snarling and screeching. Eyes wide, Rachel started toward her with the gladius, its blade still slick and drooling blood.

Andrea turned as she reached one of the mammoth's tusks, yanking her elbow back and reaching up high. The chain snapped taut as she threw it over the great ivory loop of the tusk and wrapped it around itself. It wouldn't hold long, but she didn't need it to.

'Look out!' Rachel yelled. Instinctively Andrea dropped to the ground, letting go of the chain as a bony fist punched hard into the air where her head had been. She tumbled onto her back, looking up as it bore down on her, blood flying from its mouth like spittle, reaching—

The chain snapped it back, its grabbing claws inches from her face.

Andrea yelled, scuttling back, scrambling to her feet and dipping out of the way of another blow. The mummy was restrained by its neck, tethered to the mammoth's tusk. The whole carbon fibre body of the full-scale beast wobbled as the mummy writhed and snapped, bellowing from deep in its bony gut.

Not enough, Andrea realised, it wasn't enough to hold it, not long enough for what she had planned. Drawing in a deep breath, she ducked toward it and reached for the loose length of chain still hanging from its collar.

'Come here, you undead freak—'

Claws thrust into her eye and she yowled in pain, tipping back as a burst of warmth sprayed her cheek.

She doubled over, a thick wet bolt of agony pulsing through her head. Clutching at her eye she looked up through a sea of red mist to see the mummy tugging and yanking against the chain, the tusk it was tethered to starting to crack—

Rachel slammed her body into the mummy's chest and grabbed the loose chain from its neck, snapping it toward the other tusk and looping it over.

'Yes!' Andrea screamed, stumbling forward as Rachel pulled the chain taut over the second tusk. The mummy bent and pulled against the chains but it was shackled now, the chains pulling it in two directions, the great curled tusks either side of its body splintering but not breaking, not yet. The sword clattered to the ground as Rachel grunted with effort, using both hands to wind the chain around the mammoth's thick ivory horn.

Heart pounding in her chest, her left eye screaming red hot, Andrea darted forward and grabbed the sword by the hilt. It was heavy, meant for one hand but horribly balanced, the blade wide and short but sharp, that was the main thing, brilliantly sharp and glinting blue in the light.

The mummy roared, splaying both its hands wide, and a terrible green light flared like electricity in the depths of its eye-sockets. Emerald-green embers sparked beneath the cracks in its skull, a thin jade mist seeping between its ribs, between its spread fingers.

'Andrea…' Rachel moaned, her eyes on the space behind the older woman.

Slowly, Andrea turned her head to look.

Green sparks flickered in the eyes of the nearest body as it began to twitch.

Bruce was convulsing, his chest heaving as more blood bubbled out of it. The same bright light burned in his face, his knee shooting up suddenly as if somebody had tapped it with a hammer.

Andrea's eyes widened as Brother Fletcher's hands jerked stiffly, fingers curling into claws. Across the room, Arkham's head started to turn toward her, his stomach wrenching, contracting, whole body shuddering in its robes.

The power to bring the dead to life…

'Well, that's quite enough of that,' Andrea murmured, and she turned and raised the sword high.

She swung it hard with both hands, slamming the blade into the side of the mummy's skull. There was a sick *crack!* as the heavy blade smashed into the mess of bone beneath its jaw and ploughed all the way through, separating the creature's head from its neck and batting it across the room. A thick cloud of black dust exploded from the mummy's shoulders and it slumped, headless, to the ground.

Andrea drew in a deep breath, staggering back, glancing toward the archway. The bodies had gone still again, all the green light vanished from them.

'Jesus fucking Christ,' she breathed.

Rachel sunk back from the mammoth's tusk, the chain slipping from her hands and piling up loudly on the floor beside the headless mound of bone.

It was over.

'You okay?' Rachel whispered.

Andrea looked across at her through her good eye, the other pulsing wetly in its socket. The adrenaline would fade soon, and she would feel the pain – really feel it. For now, she was content not to be completely blind. Her breathing ragged, she nodded exhaustedly. 'Fine,' she lied. 'You?'

Rachel nodded back. 'Fine.'

Andrea dropped the sword with a loud clatter and reached out a hand. 'Let's get out of here,' she said quietly.

Rachel stepped forward, took her hand. Andrea squeezed it, grimacing as her brain shuddered painfully. 'We need to get you to a hospital,' Rachel said. She looked concerned. *Very* concerned, Andrea noted reluctantly, starting to feel a little sick. It must have been bad.

'Come on,' Andrea said, leading the girl toward the archway. Careful to avoid stepping near any of the bodies, she headed for the light of the foyer and tried not to think about Bruce. Or what the hell she was going to tell his mother. Oh, god. Oh, *god*. Oh…

Behind them, something clacked. Bone on bone,

joints wriggling.

Andrea turned her head, eyes wide and fearful. Between the mammoth's tusks the sprawled carcass of the mummy reached blindly for its head, claws clicking together as it crawled forward—

There was a loud *crunch* as Rachel stomped her heel hard into the bony plates of the creature's skull. It caved in under her foot and the body slumped again.

'Guess we'd better get it back in its box,' Andrea said, and Rachel nodded wordlessly.

Chapter 16

The exhibition hall upstairs was carnage. Bodies in orange robes lay scattered among shattered glass and tipped exhibits, blood spattering the walls.

The sarcophagus was still open when they dragged the mummy's cold, lifeless carcass into the hall. Its great grey lid was tipped on one side, a thin black crack splintering it from one side to the other.

They reached the sarcophagus and Andrea began to cry softly, cradling the mummy's smashed head in her arm, gripping the lip of the box with her free hand. Her knuckles whitened as she bent forward, suddenly wracked with emotion.

Poor Jez was still in there, broken and bloody, snapped out of shape.

'I don't think this exhibition is opening tomorrow,' Rachel said quietly from the door, the rest of the mummy slumped beside her in a rotten grey pile.

'We'll be lucky if the museum can open at all,' Andrea murmured, sniffling and wiping her nose with the back of her sleeve. 'Tomorrow or any other day.'

Gingerly, she dropped the skull into the sarcophagus and stepped back.

'At least it was only us here,' she said.

'Yeah,' Rachel said. 'What are the… what'll the police think about that?'

A switch snapped on in Andrea's mind and she snapped back to reality. Christ. The police. What the hell were they going to do when they showed up here? 'What are they going to do to us?' she whispered.

'We can't very well tell them it was an ancient mummy,' Rachel said. 'They'll never believe us.'

So many bodies, Andrea thought. God, they were surrounded by death. And Rachel was right, there was no hope of trying to tell them the truth…

'I don't know,' she said. 'I don't know what to do.'

Somewhere in the building, somebody shrieked.

Andrea burst through the door to the curator's office and froze.

Dr Irene Curran sat behind the desk, completely still. Her left arm was gored to a stump, and had been half-reasonably bandaged with a ragged blouse. It might have been the spare beige one that Irene kept in the office, but Andrea couldn't tell for sure; it was saturated crimson. The curator's throat and chest were savaged, rent deeply with thick, dark gashes. Her hair was matted with blood.

Phillips stood at her shoulder, holding the sharp, glinting blade of a letter opener to Curran's throat. He was grinning madly, blood in his teeth, eyes wide with desperation.

'Mum,' Andrea said, swallowing back tears. 'I'm so sorry. I didn't know you were here…'

Curran smiled weakly, her own eyes wet. She was pale, almost white, draining more blood every second. Her chest heaved as she breathed shallow, rasping breaths.

'You bastard,' Andrea seethed, turning on Phillips. Behind her Rachel stood helplessly in the doorway, a hand over her mouth. 'She needs to go to hospital, for god's sake. What the hell are you doing?'

'They promised me everything,' Phillips hissed. 'I only came here to make sure they saw it through. Now… it was all for nothing, Andrea. All of it. And I need something from your mother. I need a guarantee. Something to show for all this.'

'You want her to promise she won't fire you?' Andrea said, incredulous. 'Christ, Phillips, everyone in this building is probably out of a job now! Dozens of people are dead upstairs, you understand? And this is all you can think about?!'

'This is all there is,' Phillips said. 'Security. Nothing else matters.'

'You're a fucking idiot,' Andrea said.

'A guarantee,' Phillips insisted, pressing the blade to Curran's throat. New beads of blood welled at the edges of her wounds, drizzling softly down her neck. 'Now.'

'All right,' Rachel said quietly from the doorway.

Andrea stepped to one side and Rachel moved into the room, holding her phone aloft. There was a soft *click* as she jabbed a button with her thumb, and then another.

'I guarantee you we'll send this to the police,' Rachel said, turning the phone to show him. On the screen, a photograph of Phillips, bloody and bedraggled, holding the blade to Curran's chin.

'That's my girl,' Andrea whispered, neither of them mentioning Rachel's lack of service. It didn't seem worth bringing up, somehow.

Phillips whitened. 'You're here too,' he whimpered, glancing down at the gladius in Andrea's hand. 'And your fingerprints are *all over* that thing.'

'Oh, this?' Andrea said, stepping forward suddenly. The room swam as her vision filled with red. Phillips staggered back, withdrawing from Curran's seat. 'I can take this with me when we leave. And we are leaving, right now. We're going to the hospital. And you'll be right here when the police come, ready to answer any questions they have.'

Phillips shook his head. 'CCTV,' he said. 'It'll show you—'

'I think the monks might have taken care of that already,' Rachel said.

'She might have a point,' Andrea said, smiling thinly. 'After all, they did come to rob the place.'

'Then I'll tell them,' Phillips said. 'I'll tell them all of this was you.'

'Oh, I'm sure you will. And I'm sure they'll have *dozens* of questions. How could they not? But we'll have figured out a story of our own by then.'

She raised the gladius, pointing it at Phillips' throat, hoping he'd get the message before the weight of it made her arm sag. She was exhausted, beaten, useless. But she only needed him to believe that she was all right for a few seconds.

Raising his hands, Phillips dropped the letter opener to the floor and nodded. 'Fine,' he whispered. 'Go, then. Let's just see who they believe.'

Stepping around Curran's office chair, Andrea slowly lowered the sword and laid a soft hand on her mother's shoulder. 'Ready?' she said gently.

Curran nodded weakly.

'Give me a hand, Rach?'

'Gladly.'

Together they wheeled Curran's office chair out of the room, Andrea never taking her eyes off the man cowering before them. When they were in the corridor she reached for the door, smiling back at him before slamming it closed.

She went to her mother, fumbling in her bloody jacket for her keys. 'The honours?' she said, offering them to Rachel. The girl nodded, taking them and dipping behind her to lock the office door.

Andrea crouched before Curran's chair, laying a hand on her good arm. 'I didn't know you were here,' she said tearfully, her voice barely a whisper. 'I'm so sorry. I didn't know any of this would happen.'

Curran smiled weakly, lifting her good hand, taking Andrea's in it. 'It got your eye…' she rasped.

'It got more of you,' Andrea said gravely. 'We need to get to A&E. About an hour ago.'

'Would've killed me…' Curran whispered. 'Somebody started shouting. Downstairs… sounded like your man. That Bruce. Came in through the… back… started calling for you.'

Andrea swallowed. 'He saved your life,' she realised.

Curran nodded lightly, cringing as pain seared the stump of her arm.

'Right, let's get out of here,' Andrea said, standing straight. 'It'll be light soon. We don't want to be anywhere near here by then.'

Curran grabbed her by the skirt, tugged sharply.

Andrea looked down.

'The museum…' Curran whispered.

'I don't know,' Andrea said softly. 'I'm sorry. After this…'

Curran shook her head. 'That's all right. That's all right. All that matters… is that you're… that we're…'

'Yeah,' Andrea said. Rachel came up beside her and she smiled at the younger woman. 'We're all okay. And whatever the fuck any of this was… we'll figure the rest out as we go.'

Epilogue

The foyer was still.

Grey haze crept up the pillars as the front windows flooded with light, a pale glow catching on the dust in the air and lilting over the reception desk, which amazingly had only been shunted an inch or so out of place in all the fury of the creature's rampage through the museum. There was an uneasy calm about the lobby, a thickness in the air that felt pregnant, ready to burst, to ignite somehow and unleash a pulsing wave of heat through the building. But it didn't, even as the sun rose on the square outside and crowds began to thicken outside. The air just hung, silent, effortlessly threatening.

Blood pooled down the steps of the grand stone staircase, running from the disembowelled stomach of an orange-robed body sprawled against the banister. Thick trails of red slid down each step and gathered wetly on the next until the garish crimson paint reached the floor.

Upstairs, more bodies lay in the corridors, broken and beaten, bloody. Mangled, crushed mouths shrieked silently, wide eyes filled with red mist. The calm of the foyer seemed to spread up here like a cloud, enveloping everything.

Nothing moved.

In one of the exhibition halls, a display called Mysteries of the Ancient World had exploded into a chaos of glass and blood, antique artefacts littered among the twisted carcasses the mummy had left in its wake. The walls were spattered with red and showered with chunks of glass and rubble; one of the windows was shattered, and as a thin breeze drifted into the hall it lifted the robes of the corpses farthest from the door, giving some life to the unnaturally still collection of bodies.

The galleries were still, empty; with no visitors to wander the halls, the museum was little more than a hollow shell, a husk of limestone and priceless things. A twitching pile of bones in the Hall of Pleistocene Mammals lay among the lifeless, glass-eyed creatures displayed there. Somewhere in the square, a siren warbled loudly, the screams growing shriller and shorter as it came nearer, the sound muffled inside by layers of stone.

A small room on the second floor was alive with a rapturous explosion of noise, the walls almost trembling as something inside pounded and hammered

– not just something but a number of somethings, a cacophony of fists and heads smacking the stone in which they had been trapped.

The Ancient Egyptian Rites exhibit was filled with glass cabinets, a broad stone sarcophagus inside each one surrounded by the artefacts which had accompanied its inhabitant to the afterlife; now all those ancient coffins were trembling, shuddering with every impact as the things inside moaned and roared and bellowed, lungs thousands of years old but imbued with new breath. In a cabinet in the corner of the room a scrawny, bandaged cat paced the felt floor of its display, blind and voiceless but frantic, its gauze-covered hackles raised, its tail brushing the glass as it stalked the tiny space behind it.

In the centre of the room, a mummy propped on iron rods roared as it bent and twisted on the display apparatus buried in its back and legs, arms and upper body jerking dreadfully as its exposed, gurning maw opened in a maddening and rage-filled scream. Green lights flared behind the gauze covering its eyes.

The lights flickered as a pane of glass shattered, the ancient lid of one of the sarcophagi finally tilting forward and toppling into the room in a spray of glinting shards. A brilliant emerald light blazed inside the coffin as something inside it lurched forward, the broken frame of something long-dead bending its arms impossibly, spreading its fists into claws.

A long, terrible screech echoed through the museum.

Another glass case smashed, and then a third.

Outside, the sun continued to rise, drawing gentle fingers across the roof of the building and extending its shadow across the square.